"Dianna! You're bleeding!"

She didn't recall falling to her knees, but that was where she was, gasping, when Travis found her. Only then did she notice the blood on her hand.

"I'm all right," she managed, her throat aching. "I got free. I scratched Farley's face."

"Farley? He was here?"

Before she could respond, she was lifted to her feet, but the wobbliness of her legs didn't matter, for Travis pulled her firmly against his chest. This time she didn't mind being held tightly by a man.

This time it was Travis.

"You're okay?" he murmured softly into her hair.

"He tried to choke me. Why now? He could have killed me before, if he'd wanted to."

She gave a small cry of protest as Travis pulled back to inspect her. Very gently, his fingers touched her throat.

"Damn him," he said. "I swear, you're not leaving my sight. Ever again." The steely look on Travis's face made it clear he meant it. She had the sudden feeling Travis would risk his very soul to make sure Farley got what he deserved.

Dear Harlequin Intrigue Reader,

We've got an intoxicating lineup crackling with passion and peril that's guaranteed to lure you to Harlequin Intrigue this month!

Danger and desire abound in *As Darkness Fell*—the first of two installments in Joanna Wayne's HIDDEN PASSIONS: Full Moon Madness companion series. In this stark, seductive tale, a rugged detective will go to extreme lengths to safeguard a feisty reporter who is the object of a killer's obsession. Then temptation and terror go hand in hand in *Lone Rider Bodyguard* when Harper Allen launches her brand-new miniseries, MEN OF THE DOUBLE B RANCH.

Will revenge give way to sweet salvation in *Undercover Avenger* by Rita Herron? Find out in the ongoing NIGHTHAWK ISLAND series. If you're searching high and low for a thrilling romantic suspense tale that will also satisfy your craving for adventure—you'll be positively riveted by *Bounty Hunter Ransom* from Kara Lennox's CODE OF THE COBRA.

Just when you thought it was safe to sleep with the lights off…*Guardian of her Heart* by Linda O. Johnston—the latest offering in our BACHELORS AT LARGE promotion—will send shivers down your spine. And don't let down your guard quite yet. Lisa Childs caps off a month of spine-tingling suspense with a gripping thriller about a madman bent on revenge in *Bridal Reconnaissance*. You won't want to miss this unforgettable debut of our new DEAD BOLT promotion.

Here's hoping these smoldering Harlequin Intrigue novels will inspire some romantic dreams of your own this Valentine's Day!

Enjoy,

Denise O'Sullivan
Senior Editor
Harlequin Intrigue

GUARDIAN OF HER HEART

LINDA O. JOHNSTON

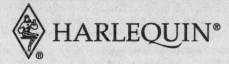

HARLEQUIN®

TORONTO • NEW YORK • LONDON
AMSTERDAM • PARIS • SYDNEY • HAMBURG
STOCKHOLM • ATHENS • TOKYO • MILAN • MADRID
PRAGUE • WARSAW • BUDAPEST • AUCKLAND

ISBN 0-373-22757-4

GUARDIAN OF HER HEART

Copyright © 2004 by Linda O. Johnston

Visit us at www.eHarlequin.com

Printed in U.S.A.

ABOUT THE AUTHOR

Linda O. Johnston's first published fiction appeared in *Ellery Queen's Mystery Magazine* and won the Robert L. Fish Memorial Award for "Best First Mystery Short Story of the Year." Now, several published short stories and novels later, Linda is recognized for her outstanding work in the romance genre.

A practicing attorney, Linda juggles her busy schedule between mornings of writing briefs, contracts and other legalese, and afternoons of creating memorable tales of the paranormal, time travel, mystery, contemporary and romantic suspense. Armed with an undergraduate degree in journalism with an advertising emphasis from Pennsylvania State University, Linda began her versatile writing career running a small newspaper, then working in advertising and public relations, later obtaining her J.D. degree from Duquesne University School of Law in Pittsburgh.

Linda belongs to Sisters in Crime and is actively involved with Romance Writers of America, participating in the Los Angeles, Orange County and Western Pennsylvania chapters. She lives near Universal Studios, Hollywood, with her husband, two sons and two cavalier King Charles spaniels.

Books by Linda O. Johnston

HARLEQUIN INTRIGUE
592—ALIAS MOMMY
624—MARRIAGE: CLASSIFIED
655—OPERATION: REUNITED
688—TOMMY'S MOM
725—SPECIAL AGENT NANNY
757—GUARDIAN OF HER HEART

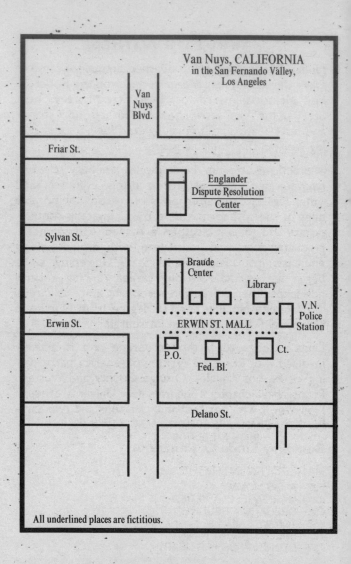

Van Nuys, CALIFORNIA
in the San Fernando Valley,
Los Angeles

Van
Nuys
Blvd.

Friar St.

Englander
Dispute Resolution
Center

Sylvan St.

Braude
Center

Library

V.N.
Police
Station

Erwin St.

ERWIN ST. MALL

P.O.

Fed. Bl.

Ct.

Delano St.

All underlined places are fictitious.

CAST OF CHARACTERS

Dianna Englander—She misses her murdered husband, but will never again allow so domineering a man into her life.

Travis Bronson—The undercover cop got distracted on his last case by caring too much, and the civilian he was protecting got killed. He has vowed that won't happen again.

Glen Farley—He learned the sweetness of revenge by murdering Dianna's powerful politician husband—the first of many. But why is he tormenting Dianna again?

Julie Alberts—The adolescent's mother died in an accident last year, and she has grown close to her "aunt" Dianna.

Jeremy Alberts—Julie's father and one of Dianna's bosses, he wants more from Dianna than her excellent work managing the dispute resolution center named for her deceased husband.

Wally Sellers—Jeremy's partner is eager to obtain publicity for the Englander Dispute Resolution Center. Too eager?

Bill Hultman—The restauranteur would do nearly anything to increase business.

My thanks to the wonderful men and women
of the Los Angeles Police Department,
especially those who were so kind in answering my
questions and giving me a tour of the Van Nuys station
for this book. I admit to modifications and exaggerations
in the interests of my story.

My thanks also to *my* wonderful man, Fred.

Prologue

Dianna Englander drew in her breath so sharply that it sounded like a muffled scream.

There. Behind the green minivan, several rows away in the parking garage, stood a familiar figure. Again.

He was too far off for her to see him clearly, but she felt him grinning at her.

She stood, trembling, beside her red sports car in its assigned parking space. She gripped the handle of the driver's door. Moisture flooded her eyes and spilled over—tears of fury. Of frustration.

Of anguish.

She'd known she hadn't been hallucinating the first time she'd seen him, a week earlier.

After all this time, he had come after her. *Here.*

Oh, she hadn't been hard to find after all the hype about the opening of the Englander Dispute Resolution Center almost exactly a year ago.

The Center had been named after her husband Brad— dead, thanks to the man who stood just a few yards away. Murdered by that monster.

And so was the precious baby created by Brad and her, who had died before ever being born...

"Damn you, Glen Farley." Dianna's voice was barely

a whisper, but it echoed in her mind. *Damn you...
damn you.*

But she was the one who had been damned.

Knowing how foolish it was, she took a step toward
the evil creature who had ruined her family. He raised
his hand as if waving to her and walked beyond the
minivan and into the next row of parked vehicles.

"Stop!" She hadn't intended to cry out, but the shout
filled the air.

She heard soft voices behind her and turned. A
woman with a couple of kids approached a sedan a few
cars away, looking nervous as she hastily shepherded the
children inside.

Dianna pasted a small smile on her face that she intended to be reassuring. But judging by the way the
woman slammed her car door shut and quickly started
the engine, Dianna knew she looked as distraught as she
felt.

As the car pulled away, she returned her attention to
where she had seen Farley.

He wasn't there.

She realized then how fast she was breathing. Inhaling
the ugly odor of exhaust fumes, here in the indoor parking garage.

She yanked at her purse until its strap jerked off her
shoulder. She fumbled with the zipper till it opened and
dug for her cell phone. *Call 9-1-1,* the rational part of
her mind instructed.

"Hey, Dianna," said a soft female voice behind her.
Dianna pivoted. Eleven-year-old Julie Alberts stood near
her father Jeremy's black luxury sedan in its space two
over from Dianna's. Julie's brown eyes, luminous even
in the dim parking garage light, widened. Tendrils of
brown hair that had escaped from the barrette at the back

of her neck framed her gamine face in coiled wisps. "Are you okay?" she asked.

No! Dianna wanted to scream. But she didn't want to frighten Julie. "I'm fine, honey. I was just leaving. Get in my car and come with me, okay?" She slipped her phone back into her purse. What good would the police do now?

"But my dad's supposed to meet me here to drive me home."

But Farley was here. Farley killed people.

They had to leave, all of them.

"We'll pick him up at the elevator," Dianna said. "Let's go. Now."

Julie didn't move. She looked scared. "Dianna, what's wrong?"

Before she could answer, Jeremy Alberts appeared near the doorway from the elevator. "There he is." Dianna motioned to him to come quickly, then hesitated. Was it better to flee through the garage or drive out? Before she made up her mind, Jeremy joined them. "What's wrong?" he demanded, parroting his daughter's words. He gave Dianna an odd look.

Her emotions were clearly showing.

"Did you see—?" He didn't finish, but the question remained written in the furrow of his shaggy salt-and-pepper brows.

He didn't have to say more.

Dianna had filled him in the first time. Fortunately, he had believed her. Had acted appropriately.

But all his security measures hadn't stopped Farley from returning.

"We'll fix it, Dianna," he said in a gruffly reassuring voice. "Don't worry."

"We need to get out of here," Dianna told him. "Now."

"Yes," he agreed, hurrying Julie to his car.

Dianna tried to watch everywhere at once. There were no other cars driving around, no further sign of Farley. But that didn't mean he wasn't still here. Or that he hadn't rigged up something harmful.

"What's going on?" Dianna heard Julie insist before the car door closed behind her.

Dianna got into her own vehicle. Her hands trembled as she clutched the steering wheel, and she watched all around as she let Jeremy's car lead the way down the ramp, get out first.

If Glen Farley hurt someone else, it shouldn't be the Alberts.

Or her. Or anyone.

It had been more than a year since he'd stopped stalking her…before.

Why was he here? Oh, Lord, why was he here?

Chapter One

"Why is it that you're always hungry after school?" Dianna gave Julie's shoulders a hug as the elevator door opened onto the vast, architecturally dynamic lobby of the Englander Dispute Resolution Center. The building was modern, yet, with its arched windows, high ceilings and sparkling chandeliers, its feel was old-world grand.

The heels of Dianna's navy pumps clicked on the marble floors. The shoes matched her linen suit—short-skirted, professional but comfortable in the Los Angeles winter. Dianna, from the east, still couldn't get used to how warm it was this time of year. She had even cut her blond hair into a soft, slick pageboy parted in the middle, rather than keeping it long as she had once worn it.

Or maybe she'd needed to change everything about her life....

"Being bored at school starves me," the child replied to Dianna's question, looking up with a huge, adult-charming grin that displayed slightly crooked front teeth.

She kept grinning even as, on their way to the door outside, Dianna and she passed by the security guards screening people who entered.

Dianna kept grinning, too—but hers was forced.

She had Jeremy, Julie's father, to thank for the extra security in the building. Of course, since this was part of the Van Nuys, California, civic center, security screening was a way of life. The area housed all sorts of government office buildings: federal, state and municipal. And courthouses. And post offices. And other structures that could attract unsavory people with mayhem on their minds.

Like Glen Farley.

But these dark-uniformed, brusque security guys were new. Efficient, thorough and even unnerving, they had come highly recommended, Jeremy had said, by some law enforcement hotshots he trusted. He had hired them as a result of Dianna's spotting Farley the first time. He hadn't seen the horrible man. Neither had Julie. But thank heavens Jeremy had taken her word for it. She had nearly given up hoping for people to believe her.

She certainly hadn't bothered notifying the feds hunting for Farley since Brad's murder, either about the first time she saw Farley here or the second. During those initial horrendous months after her husband's death, she had seen Farley several times, hanging around. Taunting her. She'd reported it then. But the agents on the case had evidence that Farley had fled the area —evidence they apparently found more credible than her fearful and emotional phone calls. Though they claimed to have checked, they'd found no sign of him.

The last times she called, she doubted they'd looked at all.

That was one of many reasons she had left Washington.

"Hey, look," Julie said, drawing Dianna out of her disturbing thoughts. She pointed her index finger, its nail chewed to an irregular edge, toward a pushcart on the paved plaza outside the Center.

One day, Dianna would have to introduce the girl she thought of as her surrogate niece to the pleasures of nail polish—clear or light pink, for a preteen. Maybe then she wouldn't gnaw on her nails.

Julie didn't have a mother to teach her such things.

"What's that guy doing?" Julie grabbed Dianna's elbow and pulled her toward the elaborately decorated cart. A sign on its surface proclaimed that it sold "Fare to keep you awake and alive." Below was a list of food, drinks and prices: mochas, lattes and all imaginable coffee creations, sweet rolls, and cold gourmet sandwiches.

Dianna hadn't thought she was hungry, but her stomach grumbled.

What *was* that guy doing?

A man in a white T-shirt with a red Cart à la Carte logo in the middle stood right beside the pushcart. His hands were in motion—a good thing, too, for he was juggling knives. And not wimpy butter knives, but steak knives with wicked-looking serrations. He wasn't tossing them high, but they flew end-over-end as he flawlessly caught and tossed them in his obviously skilled, large hands. The motion of his arms emphasized the breadth of substantial biceps and tautened his shirt against his equally broad and muscular chest.

"Wow," said Julie in an awed voice beside Dianna. *I'll second that,* Dianna thought, though for different reasons than Julie. The guy was definitely sexy.

Not that she was into guys these days, let alone sex. It was okay to admire a good looking man from afar, but that was definitely all.

This guy's hair was sandy brown, cut short, almost military style. He was barely even looking at the dangerous utensils that twisted and soared under his control. His cobalt-blue eyes appeared to be fixed on Dianna.

And when she caught his glance, one corner of his wide, straight mouth curved slightly upward in acknowledgment.

She had seen him before.

Where?

He stopped juggling, catching the knives and setting them down on the cart. "Can I help you?" he said. "How about an albacore tuna sandwich for the young lady, and an espresso for her lovely companion?"

The guy's tongue was as flawless as his juggling. As he'd stressed the word *young,* Dianna had been certain he would refer to her as the "older lady," but instead he had complimented her.

She recalled suddenly where she had seen him before: in the reception area of the A-S Development offices, where Dianna managed the dispute resolution center named for her husband.

The Englander Center was an experiment that held great promise, and A-S Development, which had constructed it, also was responsible to ensure its use.

In this area abounding with courts and litigants, the idea was to encourage people to save time and money by paying mediators to help them resolve disputes amicably. Or, if they couldn't, they could hire "rent-a-judges"—real, retired judges who held realistic trials in the Center's own model courtrooms.

So far, the experiment was a success. The law offices within the Center were completely rented, and Dianna had no problem filling the conference and courtrooms nearly constantly.

So many people were undoubtedly a good market for food vendors. And that was where Dianna had seen the gorgeous hunk of a juggler before: that morning, in her office, peddling food.

"Would you like a sandwich here, Julie?" she asked the girl. "Or would you like to go to one of the other carts along the promenade?"

"Oh, but you have to stay here," the man told them. "It's in the cards." Dianna couldn't figure out where he could have fit a deck of cards in the side pocket of his snug jeans, but he whipped one out with a flourish. "Pick a card, lovely companion," he said, stepping toward Dianna.

She felt her cheeks redden. "No, thanks," she said. "Julie, let's—"

"Please, Dianna," the girl begged, excitement glimmering in her eyes.

"Well…" Dianna turned back toward the man and shrugged. "All right."

She put out her hand, mentally comparing it with Julie's much smaller one. Her nails were rounded, and she used a rose-tinted polish.

The man fanned out the cards. "Go ahead," he said as she hesitated. "Pick one."

Dianna closed her thumb and forefinger on one from the middle of the deck. She pulled it out.

"Now look at it," the man said.

She did, then blinked, unable to believe her eyes. It was a three of clubs. But it wasn't the suit or the number that startled her.

Printed along the card's side was, "Beware."

LT. TRAVIS BRONSON, of the special Undercover Response Unit, "L Platoon," of the Metro Division, Los Angeles Police Department, did not let himself smile at the reaction of the beautiful, slender, but unapproachable woman he knew was Dianna Englander, widow of U.S. Representative Bradley Englander.

He had intended to startle her. It was the best way to get her attention.

"Now, please place the card back into the deck," he told her. Her slim, elegant hand trembled as she obeyed. But she lifted her pale blue eyes to his and glared.

Brave lady, he thought.

"Watch," he said. Using simple sleight-of-hand, he formed the cards back into a solid deck, shuffled them, then easily extracted the one Ms. Englander had selected: the three of clubs.

He knew why she had reacted so strangely. It had a warning on the edge. But so did all the cards in the deck he had proffered.

"Is that the one you chose?" he asked.

She nodded. "Of course, but you—"

"Now, how about that tuna sandwich, my friend?" He knelt to the level of the child he knew to be Julie, daughter of Jeremy Alberts, a developer of the building near where they stood.

"Sure," said the girl, wonder written all over her enormous-eyed gaze. He was careful to make sure she hadn't seen what was on the card.

"I'll teach you how to do that someday, if you'd like," he said.

"Really?" Her tone told him that she considered what he had offered a gift of the highest magnitude.

To him, card tricks, juggling and other feats with his hands were routine.

Ms. Englander appeared less impressed.

"Manny, would you get our young customer her sandwich?" he asked the thin Hispanic man who actually owned the pushcart. Manny Fernandez nodded and motioned to the child.

That gave Travis his opportunity. He reached into his pocket, but she gave him no time to show his badge. Instead, she muttered, "I don't know what he paid you, but leave me alone. And if you're smart, you'll stay away from him, too." She turned her back and followed the child. "Let's go, Julie," she said after she paid Manny, then turned back toward the building.

He wasn't going to argue with her…here. But this wasn't the end of it, especially because Travis could guess what "he" she referred to. "See you soon," he said as she and the child passed.

She spared him barely a look. "Don't count on it," she said through gritted teeth.

Oh, but you can count on it, Ms. Englander, he thought.

He watched the woman and child disappear through the doors.

A SHORT WHILE LATER, Dianna forced herself to sit still in Wally Sellers' office in the A-S Development suite, on the sixth floor of the Englander Center.

Wally, chubby and unkempt but happy in his own cascades of loose skin, had decorated his domain in a manner in keeping with his unassuming nature: mismatched but comfortable stuff. He sat behind his cluttered desk.

"I'm glad we're meeting," Dianna said. "I have something to tell you both, but I'll wait till Jeremy gets here. Do you know what he wants to see us about?"

Almost as soon as Julie and she had walked back into the offices, her other boss, Jeremy Alberts, had told her they had to get together on an important matter. Though their meeting would be short, as Wally and he had some potential subcontractors coming in, they would convene now in Wally's office.

Dianna had tried to take Jeremy aside to tell him about her fright in the plaza but hadn't wanted to alarm Julie. She had already alerted the security crew downstairs, told them to contact the police. If local authorities interrogated that cheeky pushcart peddler, they might get information about his relationship with Glen Farley that could lead to Farley's arrest at long last. *This* time she would not allow her claims to be ignored. She was no longer the terrified, hysterical widow whom federal agents had blown off before.

Jeremy bustled into the office, hurrying across the Berber carpet between the cluttered desk and the sitting area. "Good," he said, glancing between Wally and Dianna. "You're both here." He took a seat on an orange-and-blue upholstered chair that clashed with Dianna's blue-and-gray one, and tugged on his pants legs to arrange them. "I've settled Julie in my office doing homework. He'll be here in a minute."

"Who?" Dianna asked, but before he could respond, she continued, "Look, before whoever it is gets here, I have something I need to tell you." She related what had happened on the plaza.

"Oh, no!" Jeremy rose by his seat. "Are you okay?"

Dianna assured them both—falsely—that she was. The experience had shaken her more than she dared to admit.

Farley was getting more blatant. Now he was even hiring people to frighten her. She wouldn't know whom she could trust.

See you soon. The man's words echoed in her head. She didn't want to think about it...but how could she avoid him, if he stood right outside their building? *Beware...*

"Damn!" Jeremy said. "Well, you'll have an opportunity to tell the right person soon. The head of our new security company is coming. He demanded this meeting, said he has something important to talk about. He didn't sound happy. Maybe he already knows what's going on."

"I certainly hope so," Wally stated. He was seated again, and his scowl added creases to his wrinkly, round face.

"If he doesn't know now, we'll make sure he jumps right on it," Jeremy asserted, as usual assuming leadership.

The partnership between her bosses reminded Dianna of pairs of comedians from the past, since Jeremy was so much thinner than his counterpart. His perfectionism in business dealings carried through to his appearance, for even when he removed a tailored suit jacket, as he had for this meeting, his shirts were clearly of fine quality cottons or silks.

But the similarity to comedic teams stopped with their appearances. Though both men were kind, they tended to be serious. Neither was prone to crack jokes.

They both seemed equally rattled now.

"Look," she said placatingly. "It wasn't—"

A sound from outside Wally's office interrupted her. Beth Baines, the attractive African-American receptionist, poked her head in. "Mr. Flynn is here with another man," she said.

"Send them in," Jeremy said. "Although Cal didn't mention anyone else."

Two men entered—and Dianna rose, clenching one fist so tightly that her nails dug into her skin.

Thank heavens. The new security team had come through.

Only—was she supposed to take part in the interrogation? "No," she whispered aloud. She wanted no part of it.

One of the men, bulky and wearing a blue uniform, Dianna recognized from the group manning the metal detectors and conducting random searches of visitors at the building's entry. He was obviously a representative of the security company.

But the other—it was the good-looking juggler from the courtyard. The man who'd unnerved Dianna. He strode confidently inside, followed by Julie.

"Are you going to show us more card tricks?" the child asked, her eyes aglow once more. Dianna wanted to whisk her from the room. Julie didn't belong near this unpleasantness.

"Not now," the man said with a smile. "I've some tricks to discuss with the adults."

Tricks? Shakily, Dianna said to Julie, "Go back to your dad's office, honey, and finish your homework. I'll come help when we're done here." She gave the child a hug.

"Okay." Julie's look was baleful, but she obeyed.

The other man closed the office door behind her.

"What's going on, Flynn?" Jeremy demanded. "Who is this?"

"He's the man I told you about," Dianna said coolly. "The one who tried to scare me outside on the plaza. He must have been hired by Farley."

She glared at him, but he laughed aloud. Dianna felt her temper flare. Who *was* he?

She was able to ignore him for a moment as the uniformed man approached, holding out a hand. It felt like refrigerated meat as she shook it briefly, then let go.

"Ms. Englander." He ducked his head as if in deference. His hair was light brown, and he had a bald spot at the crown. "I should have introduced myself before. I'm Cal Flynn, president of Flynn Security. I've stationed myself right alongside my staff because of the sensitive nature of the situation. Mr. Alberts called us in after you saw Glen Farley the first time."

"That's right," Jeremy agreed. He sat again in the chair across from Dianna. "Flynn's outfit is already making a lot of changes in the Center's security."

Cal Flynn's smile broadened, revealing teeth so perfect Dianna wondered if he'd had them knocked out in the course of security assignments and replaced artificially.

Flynn continued, "Jeremy said you recently spotted the suspect a second time, and that you informed the police."

That wasn't exactly true. Dianna had mentioned it to her contact at the local police station, a community relations officer. It had been an offhand reference, but she'd told Jeremy nevertheless.

"That was fine, of course, but it would have been better if you let us handle the notification, since—"

"Since his feelings have been hurt," said the juggler. He also approached Dianna, all but shouldering Flynn aside. His hand was out, too, but not to shake hers. He held a small leather case.

Dianna took the case, then glanced up at his face in surprise as she handed it back.

It was his ID. He was Lt. Travis Bronson of the Los Angeles Police Department.

"Who is he?" Wally's voice nearly exploded from behind his desk.

Dianna told him as the police officer and security man took seats at opposite ends of the couch.

Flynn faced Lt. Bronson. "We certainly appreciate your interest and help, sir, but we have things under control."

Dianna doubted that. Farley was a murderer. And they certainly hadn't captured him.

In any event, she had a lot of questions. She asked the first. "Why were you outside juggling, of all things, Lieutenant?"

"Keeping an eye on everything," he said. "We've other guys posted around here undercover, too."

"Aren't you a bit obvious, with all your—" she wanted to say "gyrations," but that word brought back too clearly her own reaction to his sexy moves "—juggling?" she finished lamely. "And tricks."

"Ah, but what better way to draw people near so I can observe them?" The archness of his grin suggested he knew just what she had been thinking.

"But why?" Jeremy asked almost peevishly. "We've hired the best security there is. What's going on here?" He took a position beside Wally's desk. His arms were folded, and a scowl puckered his long face.

Lt. Bronson rose. He looked directly at Dianna. "Because you're in danger."

"What?" Wally drew his bulk from behind the desk and crossed to stand protectively beside Dianna. He put his hand on her shoulder. "Even if she saw Farley, that doesn't necessarily mean—"

"Oh, it means a lot," the cop said.

Dianna felt both annoyed and gratified. Wally had said *if* she saw Farley. One of her own bosses, her friend, apparently doubted her. It brought back some unpleasant memories.

But for the local police to have sent someone undercover to keep watch, they, at least, must be taking her seriously. What a relief, after being ignored so blatantly before. It felt strange, though, to think she had an ally of sorts in this irritating cop.

Dianna stood and walked toward the window behind Wally's desk. Looking down toward the courtyard, she could not see the pushcart where she had first viewed the man.

She turned back toward the sofa where he sat once more, one muscular leg crossed nonchalantly over the other in his snug jeans. The security chief sat ramrod-stiff beside him, the tight expression on his bearlike face all but shouting his annoyance.

"Why do you think I'm in danger, Lieutenant?" she asked.

"My commander got a call from Officer Treya, a community relations officer here, at the Van Nuys Station. He told me about the Englander Dispute Resolution Center, and that the late Representative Englander's widow works here. He also said you'd informed him of seeing your husband's alleged murderer here a couple of times."

"He's more than an *alleged* murderer," Jeremy contradicted. "Dianna saw him shoot Brad Englander."

Only half-conscious of the gesture, Dianna placed her hand on her abdomen. Brad was not the only victim of that horrifying scene…. "But everyone's innocent until proven guilty in a court of law," she recited in a monotone, watching a hint of amusement play in Lt. Bronson's deep blue eyes. "Right, Lieutenant?"

He nodded and stood. "But I'm inclined to believe

that an eyewitness is probably right. Which brings me back to why I'm here. Officer Treya asked a detective to look into the situation, but, as you know, Mrs. Englander, no one, not even the feds, has been able to nab the suspect. But Glen Farley's been implicated in some other situations. One was recent—the bombing of a redevelopment area in downtown L.A."

Dianna's heart rate speeded up as if she had pressed on an accelerator. "I hadn't heard that Farley was involved." She kept her breathing even. "But I'm not surprised." And that explained why, this time, she was being taken seriously.

"It's just speculation so far," the police officer said calmly. "In any event, we're placing a few strategic undercover officers to keep an eye on the Englander Center, just in case."

"Just in case what?" demanded Cal Flynn.

"Just in case he decides that one bombing in the L.A. area isn't enough. Or—" he continued, looking directly at Dianna "—if he thinks that murdering one Englander isn't enough, either."

Chapter Two

Travis almost wished he hadn't left his knives outside, locked in the cart. Juggling would help right about now.

He shoved his hands hard into the pockets of his jeans—his damn restless hands, hands that wanted to touch the lovely woman who'd gone so pale before his eyes. To help her to her chair and steady her now as she stumbled over the few steps to get there.

To hold her tight and comfort away the fear that made her gnaw, with perfect white teeth, on her lush bottom lip.

"We need you to cooperate, Ms. Englander." His voice barked more gruffly than he'd intended. She was simply another citizen. One under his protection. No one under his protection would be harmed ever again, nor would he allow himself to care about one more than others. He'd learned that lesson well. He would simply do his job. And this time, he would do it right.

"I'm sure she'll cooperate." The slimeworm Flynn was talking, a hell of a lot more placatingly than before. His turf was being invaded by the cops, and he clearly didn't like it one damned bit. But he could hardly tell the LAPD to go chase itself—at least not in so many words.

With only the slightest squaring of her slim shoulders beneath her dark suit jacket, Dianna Englander seemed to regain control. She sat, then crossed one slender ankle over the other.

Her skirt was short. Or was it that her legs were long? In either case, their endless, shapely forms tantalized Travis.

He abruptly drew his gaze back to her face. Solemnity raised her small, slightly pointed chin.

"Look, officer." Jeremy Alberts had taken Dianna's former position near the window. "Of course we'll cooperate. But we need to make sure the Center and its business aren't compromised. It's not unusual these days for buildings to have beefed up security, and we did that. But if people learn the police have us under special surveillance…well, that's different."

"Of course," Travis echoed sardonically. "We wouldn't want to compromise your business just to save a life or two."

The other guy from the building, Wally Sellers, who was walking back toward his desk chair, made a sound as if he had swallowed his spit wrong.

"That's uncalled for." Dianna Englander rose to face Travis. Her bright blue eyes were ablaze with indignation. There was no sign of her earlier fear. That, at least, was good.

"Sorry," Travis said, though he knew he didn't sound in the least chastened. "We don't intend to harm the Englander Center. There'll be less possibility of that if you cooperate."

"Of course," she acknowledged with a curt nod. "What would you like me to do?"

Travis had done his research. He knew that Jeremy Alberts and Wally Sellers were partners in A-S Devel-

opment. A-S had formed a public-private partnership
with the City of Los Angeles to build the Englander
Center at the edge of the Van Nuys civic center, to ex-
tend the redevelopment of the area. Only it wasn't called
Englander Center then. It was renamed for the U.S. Representative whose redevelopment efforts caused it to be
built after he was murdered during its construction two
years ago.

"First thing," he said, "I'd like you to give me a tour
of Englander Center."

"I'd be glad to later," Jeremy Alberts interceded, taking a step toward Travis. The fiftyish man, whose hair
had gone silver, was obviously used to being in control.
Travis wondered idly if his partner Wally ever got his
way in an argument. As between the domineering Alberts and his chubby, uneasily smiling partner, Travis
suspected Wally had his mind changed often if it dared
to hold a differing opinion. "We have people coming in
for a meeting now, but I'll show you around soon as
they're gone. Or perhaps you would like Mr. Flynn to
do it."

"Thanks," Travis said, "but I meant Ms. Englander.
I want her insight on the place, plus I need for her to
point out exactly where she thought she saw Farley."

"I'll be glad to show you where I *did* see Farley,"
she asserted. Good. She'd taken the bait. This way, she'd
insist on giving him the tour, to try to assuage any doubt
he had. And he didn't have much. If anyone would recognize Glen Farley, it was Dianna Englander.

"Fine," he said. "There's more you can fill me in
on, too."

"Like what?" Her clear blue gaze challenged him.
Though she'd said she would cooperate, she seemed to
expect him to come up with something she would refuse.

He had a feeling that, in a clash of wills between Dianna Englander and himself, he'd need a tie-breaker.

That wasn't good. Not when he had to make sure nothing happened to her, with her husband's worst enemy so close.

"I've read in the local newspaper," he said, not moving his gaze from hers, "that the Van Nuys civic center is about to have a street fair as a fund-raiser for more redevelopment."

"That's right," Dianna said. "I've been working with government agencies and local merchants to put it together."

"Security will be beefed up, too," Flynn huffed importantly. "We're already planning it, along with the private companies that support other nearby buildings."

"Any idea why that date was chosen?" Travis ignored the pompous security guy and kept his gaze firmly on Dianna's. Of course, he knew the answer.

"It coincides with the first anniversary of the opening of Englander Center," she said.

"I need to have you fill me in on the festivities," he said. "What the public has been told. Whether there's anything Glen Farley might know about the celebration, and anything he doesn't—or shouldn't—know."

"Oh." One small hand flew to Dianna Englander's mouth. "Oh, what?" Wally Sellers asked. He appeared confused.

"I wondered," Dianna said slowly, "when we first talked about the fair, if it was a good idea, but I got so caught up—"

"That you failed to consider whether some anti-redevelopment nut like Farley might consider it a challenge," Travis finished.

"What do you mean?" Wally still didn't get it. He

rose to stand beside Dianna. He was about her height, his hair black and thick, and it was hard to tell where his chin ended and his neck began. "We need good press," he continued. "A few months ago, a celebrity couple worked out their divorce settlement here, in the Center. We got such good publicity that our conference rooms are scheduled months ahead for arbitrations and mediations. We've even been booked for movie shoots in our simulated courtrooms. A big anniversary celebration will put us in the news again, bring more business. Maybe even more movie shoots."

"Farley might have come here because of the anniversary celebration, Wally," Dianna said quietly. "He may intend to do something to..." She hesitated, as if the things she contemplated as within Farley's plans were too terrible to voice.

Travis had no such compunction. "Something that would definitely get your center publicity on its first birthday," he said. "A bombing? Killing the widow of the Center's namesake? What better time than a celebration to make his perverted point?"

SINCE SEEING FARLEY the second time, Dianna had avoided parking in her designated space in the garage. She paid for valet parking, a service offered by Englander Center that allowed more visitors to stow their cars in the building's lot and added an extra touch of prestige to the dispute resolution center.

But now she was visiting her empty second-floor parking space. She ignored her apprehension. This time, she was not alone. And even if Glen Farley didn't realize that the tall, muscular pushcart peddler standing beside her was a trained—and probably armed—policeman, Dianna knew it.

She kept her voice low. "He was over there," she said to Lt. Bronson. Travis. He'd told her, before they began their tour, to call him by his first name.

In fact, he'd told her to do a lot of things. She was to cooperate. To show him around. To treat him like a pushcart peddler trying, as so many actors and others in L.A. did, to get discovered as a street entertainer, a guy who also tried to get his friends a break: showing off their skills at the anniversary celebration. His apparent attempts to convince her to hire his buddies and him would be the ostensible reason for their spending time together in the next week, as he and his fellow multi-talented officers watched over her and the Center.

And, he'd told her with determination, they *would* nab Farley.

When Travis and she reached the lobby, he told her to let him get out of the elevator first. She had been married to a man who had told her exactly what to do. Sometimes she had listened. Sometimes she hadn't, yet she'd had to give up her public relations career in favor of his political one. As a result, there had been friction between them—she'd *hated* his commands—but there had been love, too.

Except—if Brad had known when to keep his mouth shut, when not to issue commands, might he still be alive today?

And their baby—

"Let's go over exactly where you were standing, and what else you remember," Travis said. "All right, Dianna?"

She had automatically responded, when he'd said to call him by his first name, that he should use hers as well. Even though it was the norm these days not to use the more formal title of Mr., Mrs. or Ms. whatever—or, in his case, Lieutenant—she now regretted the informality. It seemed almost…well, intimate, for the two of them to be on a first name basis. And Dianna did not want to be in the least intimate with any man, particularly not an officious officer of the law—even to support his cover.

"All right, Travis." The coolness in her voice earned her a sideways look from the man who had been surveying their surroundings. Deliberately, she explained where her car had been parked both times and where she'd been standing. "The first time I saw him, he got out of a white car parked a few vehicles away in a reserved space." She shuddered at the recollection. Farley had known where she was. Why not? She'd made no secret of where she now worked—in the building her husband had once championed that now bore his name.

It was no surprise, either, that he found her in the parking garage, near her spot at the time she usually arrived for work in the morning. If he had been watching her, he would know that.

"Are you all right, Dianna?" Travis's deep voice rang with concern, and it snapped her from her reverie.

She looked up, focused on the planes of the face of the man beside her, the light shadow of beard barely showing beneath his rugged skin.

He was staring intently, as if he figured she would break.

She wouldn't. But neither would she look, right then, at the confining walls of the parking garage. The cars that could disgorge Farley at any moment.

She described the scene she'd been reliving.

"And you think Farley knew this was your space, and that you would be there then?"

She nodded. "He got out of his car long enough to

smile at me.'' She cleared her throat. "He got back in and drove away.''

"I don't suppose you got his license number."

"Part of it—a California plate that began with 4ACR.''

Travis jotted it down in a small notebook he extracted from a pocket. "Probably rented with a false ID or stolen, but we'll see if we can figure it out.''

"I'm not sure what kind of car it was, either," she continued. "It was a sedan that looked like a high-end Japanese import. But when I saw Farley again, I didn't see the same car, and that time he just seemed to disappear without driving away.''

"Okay. You're doing fine, Dianna. Now, let's go over this again." Question by question, he led her carefully through the events before, during and after both sightings of Farley, continuing to make notes.

The telling became cathartic, for when she was done, she was able to lead him to where she had seen Farley each time, without hesitation. Without fear.

Except when, in the middle of her attempt to recall what Farley had been wearing, she took a step backward and a car horn sounded right behind her. She jumped, reaching out to grasp the nearest thing she could for comfort.

It turned out to be Travis's hand.

He squeezed hers in return, pulling her out of the way by putting his other hand soothingly on her back.

Only it wasn't soothing at all. It was unnerving to have her hand held, to be caressed, by a man, a stranger, in plain view of anyone who might be watching.

It also felt much too good. It had been a long time since she had been touched and held by any man.

That's all it was, of course, her strange reaction to this

undercover cop. A perfectly human, perfectly understandable response to the touch of another human being.

The car that honked rolled by, the elderly female driver scowling as if she considered anyone near her driving lane to be in her way. Dianna shook her head in exasperation, retrieved her hand from the warm clasp of Travis's and took a few steps back.

"Look," she said, "it's not enough for you to understand what I've seen here. There's a lot more.... I don't know how much you know about Farley or what he did."

She assumed he didn't know *everything*—like the reputation she'd been burdened with—or he wouldn't be here now.

"Some. But why don't you tell me?"

As if she could compress years of anguish into a few brief sentences. But she had to try. "Do you know he once owned a small company that sold security equipment?" At Travis's nod, she continued, "He blamed my husband for putting him out of business when a redevelopment bill Brad championed was passed and the building Farley leased was torn down. He got his revenge by killing Brad. And Farley's knowledge of security—well, he's elusive. He knows what the authorities look for and how to avoid detection. But he's made sure that I've seen him."

She waited for Lt. Bronson to suggest that maybe she'd seen him too much...but he didn't. Thank heavens.

"Why?" he asked.

She waved her hand in frustration. "To scare me, I guess. But why he wants to, especially after all this time..." She shrugged. "I wish I knew."

''We'll find out when we nab him. Meantime, if you think of anything else important, let me know.''

TRAVIS HAD NO INTENTION of admiring Dianna Englander's guts.

Admiration was too close to the commencement of caring. And caring came too close to failure. And loss.

But he realized nevertheless, while he followed her slender, sexily swaying body as she hurried back toward the elevators, that he *did* admire her guts.

It didn't take a rocket scientist to figure out she was terrified by the man who'd killed her husband. But despite the traumatic recollections of seeing Farley that Travis forced her to relive, she came off cool and collected, if a little nervous.

All right, a *lot* nervous, he conceded as he watched her all but collapse against the elevator wall when they were both in the otherwise empty car.

But he'd jumped a little, too, when that impatient driver had honked a horn behind them. It had been reflex to reach out for Dianna's extended hand. Pull her back out of harm's way.

Better that than reach for the snub-nosed gun he wore in a holster at his ankle.

''Do you mind if we make a stop before we go back into the Center?'' Dianna asked as the car descended.

''Where?''

''A room in the basement. I've needed to go there for the last couple of days but haven't gotten around to it.''

''Fine,'' Travis said. She'd no doubt been too scared to visit the basement room after seeing Farley. That was smart. She shouldn't go anywhere alone right now, and the basement probably wasn't the most populated place in the Center.

She leaned past him and pushed the B button. She was near enough for a second, in that confined space, for him to inhale her scent—soft, yet definitely spicy.

Travis stepped back, to prevent himself from becoming more aware of her as a woman, and not just a person he had to protect.

He was surprised, when the door opened, to see that the basement wasn't the dreary dungeon he had anticipated. Sure, no daylight poured in since windows were nonexistent, but recessed lighting lined the hall where they emerged from the elevator.

"This way." Dianna led him past a few closed doors, then pushed open one near the end of the hall.

This was what he had figured the basement would look like.

When Dianna flicked the switch, the long room where they stood was illuminated only by bare bulbs dangling from the ceiling. Debris littered the floor—wads of old carpeting and rolls of carpet padding; coils of wire; sheets of damaged drywall; cans of obviously-opened paint, their hues evident by the cascades of color along their sides.

But when he glanced quizzically at Dianna, the light immediately seemed brightened from the glow of her smile.

"What's so special about this room?" he grumbled. Damn it, he had to stop noticing things like Dianna Englander's smile. Her scent. Her courage.

He needed distance, and not just physically. But because he could not promise himself even physical distance, he had to adopt utter detachment. Fast.

"There's nothing special about it yet." Dianna stepped farther inside and moved debris from along the wall. She paced the length, then the width, counting her steps aloud. "I just need approximate dimensions before making phone calls," she said when she was finished. "The contractors who bid will have to take more accurate measurements." She turned toward Travis. "Do cops have any imagination?"

"Probably not."

"Well, pretend. Picture this as a large playroom for kids whose parents are upstairs arguing over their custody, or over money, or over anything. This will be a haven, staffed by very special child-care personnel who are also trained therapists."

Travis frowned. "I don't think I can pretend that hard."

"You're a magician," she countered. "Consider it a feat of magic. Soft, fluffy carpets, with lots of colorful toys like blocks that kids can build with and even climb into. Bright plastic tables and chairs, with puzzles and books. Lots of light, a kitchen with fruit, juice and cookies, murals on the walls…" She was near a wall and touched it with her hand. The concrete surface was cracked. "Like I said, pretend."

The garbage on the floor was virtually colorless in the shadows. And Travis saw no kitchen.

But what he did see was a woman with vision. A very beautiful woman who enhanced *his* vision.

"Yeah," he said. "I see it."

A SHORT WHILE LATER, he insisted on accompanying her back upstairs to her office.

She hadn't wanted him to. She'd made that clear as they rode the parking lot elevator back up to the lobby, repeated it when they were alone once more in the next ascending car, in a separate elevator bank, from the lobby into the office structure.

"I'm not going to stop living just because Farley's hanging around trying to scare me," she fumed, her arms folded.

"Trying?" Travis countered. "You looked pretty damned scared to me when we first got into the parking lot."

And right about now, she just looked pretty damned *pretty*. The frown that turned her light, arched brows asymmetrical was somehow appealing.

Yeah, and maybe Travis just liked contrary women, fool that he was.

"I was a little scared," she admitted, once again proving to him that the woman had guts. "But as I said, *I'm* not about to stop living because of Farley."

He noticed how she'd stressed that *she* wouldn't stop living because of the suspect who'd shown up here. Her husband had. And, if the stories he'd read were right, so had the baby she'd been carrying.

Dianna definitely had guts.

And if Farley was the one who'd bombed that redevelopment downtown near the convention center and sports arena, and he was now around here, Travis was going to use those guts of hers, if he had to, to trap the elusive suspect. No one knew how Farley had succeeded in slipping away so many times after all the high-profile felonies he'd committed. Yet not even the feds, with all their resources, had been able to bring him in.

But Travis intended to get him. And Dianna would not be harmed. He would make sure of it.

When they got to the A-S Development suite, a couple of beefy guys who looked as uncomfortable as hell in the suits they wore were on their way out. Construction types, Travis figured, there for meetings with Alberts and Sellers.

A younger man was talking to the receptionist—what was her name? Beth? That guy seemed right at home in his suit. He also seemed right at home coming on to one woman while staring appreciatively at another. Travis didn't like the way Dianna met his gaze, but she smiled coolly and headed down the hall, Travis following in her wake.

Her office was different from the first he'd visited in this suite. The desk was a blond wood, Scandinavian in its sleekness. Across from it were two matching chairs with wooden arms, upholstered with a jagged-patterned pink-and-blue fabric that matched the taller, armless chairs around the table in her sitting area. Though there were piles of paper on the desk, they were neatly squared and, Travis had no doubt, organized.

The view from her window was, like Wally's, over the plaza below. Travis would be able to look up from his pushcart post, count windows, and know exactly where Dianna was supposed to be.

But he doubted this woman would pay attention to what he told her, even if it was for her own good.

When Dianna sat behind her desk, Travis said, "I'm going back to my pushcart, help Manny put it away for the night. That's our agreement. But I'll accompany you to your car when you're ready to go home. Call me on my cell phone." He pulled a card from his small notebook and handed it to her.

"No need," she said with a shrug. "I won't stay late, and as I told you before, I used the parking valet."

"Call me," Travis repeated, keeping his tone level. This time. But if she kept on contradicting, he would raise it till she got the message.

"I—"

She didn't get to finish her objection this time, as her office door burst open. It was Julie Alberts.

"I thought you were going to help me with my homework, Dianna," she complained. "Instead, I had to sit in my dad's office after my ride dropped me off from school and meet some of his business friends, like always." She made a face.

"Didn't your dad tell you I had to…" Dianna faltered, obviously unwilling to tell the girl that she'd had to show a cop, the man Julie believed was a juggler, where Dianna had seen a bad guy.

"He said you had some 'business to attend to.'" The singsong tone of her voice made it clear she repeated her father's words exactly.

"That's right. But I can look at your homework now, and then I'll take you home." She stared defiantly over Julie's head toward Travis, as if challenging him to contradict her.

He would have, if Jeremy Alberts hadn't come in just then. "We can all leave together," he said, looking at Dianna. But Travis knew the comment was intended for his ears as well.

The cop was dismissed. He wasn't needed by the civilians.

That was all right for tonight. After all, one of his men was under orders to follow Dianna home and surveil her home till she returned to work the next day.

But these citizens, and especially Dianna Englander, were going to learn that this particular cop wasn't about to be dismissed by them.

Not when one of them was probably in mortal danger.

Chapter Three

There were no messages on Dianna's answering machine when she got home that evening. Of course she hadn't expected any.

The machine, which sat on the vast, carved antique walnut desk in her office, was turned off.

It wasn't that she had received any threatening messages. It was all the damned hang-ups.

Which was why, after she dropped her purse onto a kitchen chair, she checked the ringer on the white wall phone near the refrigerator. It was turned off, too. The caller didn't seem to discriminate about calling when she was home or when she was gone. Or maybe he was checking her schedule.

All the more reason not to answer. Or even allow her machine to do it.

And hardly anyone had her cell phone number. She kept it off most of the time anyway, except when she was at work.

She glanced at the digital clock on the microwave oven mounted beside her stove. Dinnertime. The rumbling of her stomach had already told her that.

Her kitchen was certainly well-enough equipped for

her to prepare herself a feast. It had been the one room she had remodeled when she had bought this place.

While married to Brad, she had loved to entertain and had cooked most of their party food herself, though they could well have afforded caterers. Brad had been so proud of her that sometimes it hadn't even mattered that her life had become his.

"Don't go there," she demanded, almost startling herself by the sound of her voice in a room silent except for the refrigerator motor and muffled traffic noises from a distant freeway.

She had bought this home almost a year ago. It was located in a nice section of the San Fernando Valley— Sherman Oaks, a community next to Van Nuys, where she worked. She hadn't realized, when she bought it, that houses like this one, south of Ventura Boulevard, were considered more- prestigious, and were therefore more pricey. But she had been surprised to find a Tudor-style house in this area where mock-Spanish adobes reigned. And to find one with a Valley view... She had fallen in love with it, and, fortunately, the seller had been motivated to lower his price to one she could agree to.

She opened the freezer and extracted a frozen dinner extolled in TV ads as delicious yet healthy. The picture on its carton didn't excite her. The idea of eating yet another dinner alone, even in the home she loved, didn't excite her, either.

Maybe she should have bought a hot dog from the pushcart from that damned good-looking undercover cop....

"Shoot," she muttered aloud. She didn't want to think of Lt. Travis Bronson now. Her thoughts were turning to him much too often.

She wondered what he was doing for dinner that night…

"Shoot," she repeated, even louder.

She was always as comfortable with her own company as she was with a crowd of people. Why did she feel so lonely tonight?

Well, she didn't need to eat alone.

She called her next-door neighbor Astrid, a lawyer and single mom raising two young children alone. But Dianna knew the answer when she heard wailing in the background. "Sorry," Astrid said, "but both kids are coming down with something. I don't know which to blame for bringing it home, but I can't consider even fast food tonight." She turned down Dianna's offer of help. "I'll probably catch whatever it is, too. No need for us both to, but thanks."

Disappointed, Dianna hung up. She considered who else to call, realized why this was a bad night for each of them, then gave up. She could always stick an old movie into her DVD player and watch while she ate.

Except— "Julie," she said aloud. She'd promised the child she could call for further input on the essay she was writing for her English class.

Dianna hadn't considered before that, if she encouraged the child to call, she had to turn her phone ringer back on. She decided to call the Alberts preemptively. If they hadn't grabbed dinner on their way home, she'd suggest that she join them.

But their phone kept ringing. And *their* answering machine was not disconnected.

Dianna left a message, then resignedly turned the ringer back on her kitchen phone. She'd be able to hear it from elsewhere in her house, too.

She unwrapped the frozen dinner, stuck it into the

microwave, then headed toward the stairway to the second floor. The meal should be ready by the time she changed her clothes.

She had barely reached the stairs when she heard the phone ring. The closest extension was in the antique-laden living room. She hurried in there.

"Hello?" she said, expecting to hear Julie's breathy, childish voice on the other end, babbling about what they'd done for dinner, asking questions about her essay.

Instead, she heard only silence.

Until a click signified that the person on the other end had hung up.

A chill inched up Dianna's spine. She forced herself to walk slowly back into the kitchen, where she again turned off the phone ringer. She would call the Alberts later.

TRAVIS CHECKED IN first thing the next morning at the Van Nuys LAPD station. He had already called the undercover guy outside Dianna's house the night before. All had been quiet.

After greeting some cops he was beginning to know there, Travis went through the break room into the station's report-writing room. Empty for the moment, it was lined with narrow tables along the walls, where computers were available for any cop who needed to use them. It was a little less cluttered than many areas of the busy station.

He logged onto a computer to make some notes. When he was done printing them, he used one of the many desktop phones and called his supervisor.

Captain Hayden Lee answered on the first ring. "What have you learned so far?" he asked when Travis identified himself.

Captain Lee, of Asian descent, was head of the special "L" Platoon of the LAPD Metro Division, the undercover unit where Travis worked. He had been tapped by the Chief of Police for that assignment. Now that "L" Platoon was running as smooth as a well-maintained engine, the chief wanted to promote him to start up another new unit. But until the captain found a worthy successor, he refused to leave.

He had approached Travis to succeed him. More than once.

But, hell, Travis didn't want a damned desk job. He'd had to sit too much as a kid—that or get laughed at for his awkwardness after the accident that destroyed his family. Too many times, he'd been called "Cripple." Eventually, he'd taught himself what he'd needed to know—on his feet. Boxing. Wrestling. Football. No one laughed then.

Now, fieldwork was what he knew. Investigating crimes, catching bad guys and saving lives were what he did.

Except when he failed…

"I haven't learned much," he admitted now to Hayden. He gave a run-down of meeting Dianna Englander and the managers of the Englander Center the day before. Plus, he described the reaction of the turf-conscious private security chief Flynn.

"I'll run a check on his outfit," Lee said. "He sounds like a pain in the butt, but maybe you can find a way to use him."

"Right," Travis said. "You might also check on my request for DMV info on the beginning of a license plate." He explained that he had called one of the detectives at Parker Center, the main police headquarters in downtown Los Angeles, requesting a follow-up with the California Department of Motor Vehicles. Maybe they'd come up with a white sedan or two with license numbers beginning like the one Dianna had jotted down. Better yet, they might even find one with the owner's address in the L.A. area. Unlikely, but stranger things had happened.

"Right," Hayden said.

They'd known each other for a long time, and Hayden had helped him put together his cover for this assignment. He knew a lot of Travis's talents. And many of his flaws as well.

"Now get out there and keep the Van Nuys civic center safe for mankind, Bronson," Hayden finished. "And watch all those knives in the air."

DIANNA WENT TO WORK early that morning.

Why not? She hadn't slept much the night before. She was wide awake, despite the heaviness of her eyelids. And she certainly had plenty of work to do.

She drove upstairs into the garage and parked her prized little red vehicle in its assigned space, right beside Wally Sellers' black imported sports car that was surprisingly small, considering his girth.

Jeremy's space, on the far side of Wally's, was empty. He hadn't arrived yet, but that wasn't surprising. He always arrived later than they did, since he had to drop Julie off at school. This morning they might even be later than usual, since it had been past Julie's bedtime yesterday when she had finished her school report, with Dianna's help over the phone.

She had called the Alberts house a couple more times before reaching them. But she hadn't turned her phone ringer back on.

Still, today, for the first time in two weeks, Dianna had defiantly shunned the valet.

But she breathed a sigh of relief when the elevator door closed behind her, and she hadn't spotted Glen Farley.

There was always that evening…

"Cut it out," she whispered vehemently in the confines of the otherwise empty car. She felt her face redden as she looked around. Had the new security measures implemented by Flynn and his crew included hidden cameras in the elevator cars?

She hoped not.

Involuntarily, she glanced down at her clothes. As usual, she wore a professional-looking outfit. Today's was a deep-olive pantsuit. She wore a purse over her shoulder and carried her briefcase.

The elevator took her down to the lobby, where she needed to change elevator banks for a car that would take her up into the Center's office building.

She made the mistake of glancing out the vast expanse of glass toward the plaza outside. Sure enough, there was the same pushcart that had been there yesterday.

Travis Bronson stood beside it. A crowd had gathered around him. All Dianna could see of him was his head, for he stood taller than all the people surrounding him.

What was he doing to attract attention now? Juggling those vicious-looking knives again? She thought undercover police were supposed to be inconspicuous.

He was certainly not what Dianna would have expected, had someone told her to watch out for an undercover cop. But, then, to her knowledge she had never met an undercover cop before.

Security details, certainly. Uniformed police, bodyguards, FBI, even Secret Service—they had been part of her old life in Washington, D.C., as the wife of a U.S. Representative.

The life she had left behind, when Brad had died.

Without stopping to analyze the origin of her impulse, she pushed open one of the glass front doors and exited onto the plaza.

He seemed immediately to be aware of her, for their eyes met. For being so preoccupied with the crowd, and whatever tricks he performed for them, he was undeniably alert. And observant.

That, undoubtedly, was part of his job.

As he looked at her, a corner of his mouth curved slowly upward, as he acknowledged her with a lazy half smile.

Damn. Her pulse rate had no business speeding up like that, for no reason. Just because a too-handsome man full of his own importance smiled at her...

Forcing herself to chill out, she approached the "Cart à la Carte." The man who'd handed Julie a sandwich yesterday was busy pouring coffee, passing out sweet rolls and containers of juice— "Fare to keep you awake and alive," as written on the cart's side—and taking customers' money. What was his name? Manny?

Like many in the surrounding crowd, Manny appeared to be of Hispanic background. His smile was broad. No half grins from him. But why should he be anything but happy? He probably owned the cart, and Travis was undoubtedly drawing a huge crowd. Garnering plenty of tips, too.

Keeping her attention on the line in front of her, she waited impatiently until she reached Manny. "A medium black coffee, please," she said.

"Give her a sweet roll, too," commanded a voice

from behind her. "She looks like she needs a boost of energy this morning."

She whirled, only to find herself facing the chest of the tall man who, only a short while before, had stood beyond the cart surrounded by an audience. She hadn't been able to discern then what he was wearing. Now she could see that he was clad much as he had been yesterday: too-tight jeans and a snug T-shirt. This one was maroon instead of white, but it outlined the muscles of his chest as distinctly as the other. Quickly, she looked up into his face.

He wasn't smiling now. In fact, he seemed to regard her critically. "What's wrong?" he asked.

"Nothing," she said sweetly. "And I'll be glad to buy a poor juggler a donut or something, if you'd like, but I don't need the sugar hype."

"Then why do you look like hell this morning?"

Shocked, she glared at him, then turned away. "Now that's the way to get someone to buy more food, isn't it, Manny?"

"I think you are very pretty myself," the man said as he handed her a cup filled with aromatic coffee.

"Thanks. At least someone around here has manners." Dianna pulled money from her wallet and handed it to the real pushcart peddler. She gave him a generous tip, too. Then, without looking again at Travis, she headed for the building.

She wasn't surprised to find him at her side. She didn't even glance at him as he opened the door for her.

"See," he said. "I do have manners."

"Only when reminded."

Inside, she showed her ID card to a security man and was permitted to go through a separate line, for those who worked in the building. She scrambled to get her purse off her shoulder and put it on the metal detector's conveyor belt. Some uniformed people she didn't recognize were conducting the search of those entering the building this morning. Flynn wasn't there.

After showing a card similar to hers—not his official police ID—Travis followed her through the machinery's arch. It appeared that the apparatus was temporarily shut off—to make sure a weapon he carried did not set off the alarm?

Dianna soon found herself alone with him in the elevator car. Did this one have a camera? Would someone observe her incivility as she snubbed the undercover cop?

He didn't let her. "So, Ms. Englander, let me rephrase what I said before. As my astute boss Manny Fernandez pointed out, you are a very pretty lady."

It was her turn to give him a half smile. "Gee, thanks." But there wasn't a look of sarcasm on his face now, as she'd expected. She swallowed, as his deep blue eyes gazed unflinchingly at her. He looked earnest, damn him.

She didn't want compliments from him. She wanted him to leave her alone.

"The problem," he continued, "is that this morning you do not look as chipper as usual. As lovely." This time he grinned at her. Good. His roguishness she could deal with much better than his sincerity.

"How would you know? You only met me yesterday."

"Ah, but I've seen your picture. A lot."

She inhaled deeply. "You did your research, then."

"I always do my research." He did not seem uncomfortable alluding to his undercover job here in the elevator.

"Fine. Then you'll know I don't scare easily."

"Could have fooled me yesterday, in the parking lot." The car reached her floor and the door opened. He blocked it from closing but did not let her leave. "And this morning. What are you afraid of, Dianna?"

"What makes you think I'm afraid?" She forced her words to emerge slowly and coolly, and she painted disdain on her face as she regarded him.

"You obviously didn't sleep last night. Heavy date?"

She felt her arm tense, as if she were preparing to slap him. And she didn't do such things. "That's none of your concern." She pushed her way past him out of the elevator.

The problem was that she literally had to push him. She hadn't wanted to touch him, but he stood right in her way. As a result, she felt the substance of his arm as she shoved it aside. And then she had to edge out between his body and the protrusion of the elevator door. She tried not to touch him, but couldn't avoid it. The tips of her breasts just skimmed his chest. They responded to the contact. She felt them harden. Thank heavens she was wearing a substantial bra and opaque cotton blouse. They concealed her reaction. She hoped.

Even so, the contact wasn't lost on Travis. His half smile returned, and this time, it twinkled in his eyes.

He didn't continue to stand there but followed her down the hall. "I'd say it's very much my concern," he contradicted as she reached the door to A-S Development. "So, will you tell me what the problem is, or do I have to follow you all morning?"

She sucked in her breath. "No, thank you, Lt. Bronson," she hissed. "It wasn't anything. Just a phone call with no one at the other end."

"I see. Was that the only time?"

She sagged against the hallway wall. "No," she admitted. With a sigh, she found herself telling him of the spate of hang-ups, the myriad of non-messages on her answering machine. "I figure it's Glen Farley trying to unnerve me."

"Sounds like he's succeeding," Travis said. "Let me come in, make some calls, and we'll use his little trick against him, okay?"

Dianna didn't want to feel heartened by this man or what he said or did, but the way he took her at her word with no proof made her feel light-headed with relief. "How do we do that?"

"If we can trace those calls, we'll find him. And arrest him. And, bingo, he won't bother you any more."

She hadn't imagined she'd feel like grinning right then, but she did. "As simple as that?"

"Almost." He smiled back and they both entered the office suite.

The reception area was empty, though the door was unlocked. "Wally?" Dianna called. He didn't respond, so she looked into his office. He wasn't there. "He gets here early," Dianna said, "and opens the door. He sometimes goes back out for coffee."

"Not a good idea to keep the door open like that," Travis said with a frown.

"The Englander Dispute Resolution Center is filled with lawyers at this hour of the morning," Dianna replied with a shrug. "And even they have to go through the security check downstairs."

But a minute later, when Travis had followed her into her office, she wished she had not been so cavalier.

For there was a wrapped package right in the middle of her otherwise clear desk.

And it was ticking.

Chapter Four

Hell. Too bad Travis couldn't pull a trick from up his sleeve to deal with that.

"Oh, no. Farley." Dianna's whisper was little more than an agonized breath. Her knees appeared to buckle, and she grabbed at the closest chair.

As Travis snagged Dianna's arm to support her, he memorized the package in a glance, in case he needed to describe it later: brown paper, like a grocery bag, cellophane tape globbed all over so this present would not be easily unwrapped.

Not till it unwrapped itself. In one big ka-boom!

'Course it might not be a bomb. Yeah, it could just be a tiny teddy bear with a bad heart.

And if he believed that, he'd give the next telemarketer who called him his credit card and social security numbers.

As he studied the ticking SOB, he propelled Dianna in front of him. Not that his body would be much protection if the thing went off. "Let's get you out of here." He spoke calmly but was already shoving Dianna from the room. Fast.

She was shaking, but damned if she didn't drag her feet.

"What if it goes off? What about all the other people in the building?"

"You take care of that out in the hall. Set off the fire alarm. We need to evacuate the place."

"Okay. Sure. But what are *you* going to do?"

"Deal with the damned bomb." And he was. Indirectly. Without a hint of finesse, he pushed Dianna through her office door, out of the thankfully still-empty reception area and into the hall. He glanced quickly down the well-lighted corridor. Its off-white walls were decorated generously with wooden molding at upper and lower edges. Carved door frames matched. All attractive stuff but hardly useful... His eyes lit on the fire alarm beneath a sign heralding the emergency exit. "There." He let go of Dianna's arm and pointed toward the control box. "Set the damned thing off."

"Okay."

As she made her way in that direction, he ducked back into the reception area and picked up the phone. He had to use a land line. If the bomb was set to go off by a remote signal, he couldn't take the chance that his cell phone frequency would do the trick. He'd even shut off the computer if he'd had time, but if it hadn't set the damn thing off already, it wasn't likely to.

He thanked his lucky stars and good memory that he connected first thing with the LAPD Explosives Section. He quickly gave the particulars to the bomb tech who answered the phone.

And then he hustled into the hall after Dianna.

Fortunately, he'd completed the call to the bomb squad while he could still hear himself think. The corridor seemed plenty roomy before, but now it filled with the eardrum-shattering blare of the fire alarm. He resisted the urge to cover his ears. There were more important things for his hands to do.

People began to spill from other doors. Despite the continuing din from the alarm battering his skull, he heard irritable mutters and curses from men and women whose somber suits announced they were part of the legal profession. What, no ordinary folks, like their clients? It was probably too early in the morning, which was good. The building was less crowded.

At least now Dianna seemed steady enough to leave, only she headed for the elevator bank. "No elevator," he insisted, waving to direct the surge of people toward the emergency exit. He made sure Dianna was at the head of the line as they reached the door. The narrow but well-lighted stairwell had already begun to fill with people streaming from the two floors above.

At least the blare of the alarm was muted here, but he still felt it grate against his teeth. He ignored it, putting his hand on the back of Dianna's dark green jacket. The material felt expensive. Soft to his touch.

If just her suit gave him tactile fits, he wondered what her light hair that just skimmed the jacket's collar would feel like.

Okay, Dumbo, straighten up and do your duty. He pushed gently to propel her into the fray. This was no time to be polite and let others ahead. Not when his job was to take care of the witness who would net him Farley.

He fought his real inclination. It took every ounce of self-control to follow her downstairs. He wanted to stay, get everyone off the floor. Out of the building. Not play bodyguard to one lady, no matter how pretty she was, how soft or costly her clothes, how necessary her knowledge or powerful her connections. Or how much she appealed to each of his damned senses.

But she was the core of his mission. He'd make sure she was out and safe, and then do what he had to.

He'd make *damn* sure. Never again would someone for whom he was responsible be hurt. Or killed. Like Cassi...

If she'd only *listened* to him.

And so he followed Dianna, one hand on her slim, squared shoulder to make sure she kept moving. He stayed one step above her as they descended.

Shrill, scared voices reverberated from the stairwell walls. "Is this a drill? Why weren't we notified? Where's the fire?"

Above them all, above the blare of the fire alarm muffled by the stairwell, one strong female voice right in front of him shouted, "It's probably nothing, everyone. A suspicious package was found. We're just being cautious and getting everyone out."

The voices in the stairwell became louder, more frantic, as people relayed the message to others who hadn't heard: "Bomb!"

But Travis had to admire Dianna. Scared as she might be, she was taking charge, calming others.

Keeping her safe just might wind up being one hell of a worthwhile endeavor. And not just because she could ID Farley.

"WHAT'S GOING ON?" Jeremy Alberts demanded, maneuvering toward them, suit jacket flapping and dark leather briefcase in hand. "Dianna, are you all right? Why is everyone out here?"

Dianna and he stood across the street, catty-corner from the second newest structure in the area, with a lot of other people evacuated from Englander Center. They were more than three hundred feet away, which Travis said was the minimum evacuation area when a bomb was found. Hopefully, the Marvin Braude Center for Constituent Services wouldn't become the newest building around here again.

Dianna had also hoped, in this crowd and in the shade of the civic center buildings blocking the early-morning sun, that Jeremy wouldn't find her immediately. She hated the idea of having to tell him that the center he'd conceived of and built, that now—besides his daughter Julie—was the focus of his world, was in danger of being destroyed.

She'd been in danger of being destroyed. That wouldn't sit well with Jeremy, either.

Dianna felt laughter bubble from somewhere inside her. Realizing it would sound hysterical, she quashed it by taking a deep, calming breath. But Jeremy had made it obvious over and over that he considered her more than an employee, more than a surrogate aunt to Julie. Though Dianna had been careful never to encourage him, he might consider her expendability on a par with his beloved building.

At least Julie was another matter. His wife, Millie, was dead now, and he loved no one more than his daughter.

In any event, Dianna didn't have to answer Jeremy's questions, for he turned at the sound of sirens coming closer along Van Nuys Boulevard.

The tall, scowling man beside her had no compunction about responding to Jeremy, though. Travis didn't even keep his voice lowered, despite the throng of evacuees surrounding them. ''There was a little present on Ms.

Englander's desk this morning. Since it ticked, we decided someone else should open it.''

Hearing the murmur of voices around them segue into shocked exclamations, she glared up at him. "*We* decided?" What a stupid thing to say. She realized it the moment it left her mouth. But he hadn't allowed her a shred of choice. Despite her fear, she'd wanted to make sure others got out safely. He hadn't given her a chance. He'd simply shooed her out of there, as if she was a gnat with no mind of her own.

Yes, she reminded herself, but she'd been a terribly scared gnat, and now she was a living, unharmed one, maybe thanks to Travis.

"Pardon me." His tone was as stony as his glare. "I should have allowed you to unwrap it first, and then if you survived the blast, I'd have issued you an engraved invitation to get into an ambulance to have your bloody hands treated."

"Lovely image," she grumbled, but then added, almost apologetically, "but you're right. Thanks for getting me out of there safely."

She almost grinned at the surprise that arched his sandy brows. "You're welcome. Any time."

"No, thank you. Once was more than enough."

She met his gaze and actually did smile, in response to the sudden twinkle in his dark blue eyes. "I'll make a note of it." He was one good-looking guy when he wasn't scowling.

No, he was a good-looking guy even when he *was* scowling. But his masculine charm seemed multiplied when he relaxed, even a little.

"Dianna, tell me about that package. Was it Farley's work? You weren't hurt, were you?" Jeremy's concern jolted Dianna back to reality.

But again she didn't have to answer, for the distant sirens had grown louder, and a fleet of police cars screeched up before the building. A few of the vehicles were huge blue SUVs.

"Hey, what's happening?" asked Wally Sellers, who joined them. He was panting as if he had run to get there. "Why are the cops here? Is something wrong?"

"Bomb scare," growled his partner in a low voice.

"You're kidding." But Wally's sudden pallor showed that he believed Jeremy. Dianna worried about the chunky, out-of-breath older man. He seemed a prime candidate for a heart attack. "Where's the bomb? Does anyone know?"

"Mr. Sellers, Mr. Alberts, you okay?" Cal Flynn, head of the building's security force, joined them. His blue uniform shirt was untucked, and a sheen of sweat glistened on his round, ursine face. "I've got my guys checking the floors for fire, but so far they haven't found anything. Maybe it's a false alarm."

"Or maybe not," Travis said. "Get them out. Fast. There's something that looks like a bomb inside. The bomb disposal unit'll handle it."

Cal uttered an expletive, then yanked the radio from his belt. "I need to tell my guys to make sure everyone's out."

Travis grabbed his hand. "Great idea, but no radio. It might not make a difference out here, but if any of your guys are close to the damn thing, the radio frequency could set it off." He was pacing, as if it required every bit of self-control to keep himself from—what? Going back inside the building himself?

Dianna heard the sound of a helicopter overhead and looked up. It was close enough for her to make out the call letters of a local news radio station.

Damn! The media already knew what was happening.

"Tell you what, Flynn," Travis said, standing beside the security man. "I've got to go brief those guys on the package."

For an irritating instant, Dianna thought he was referring to the media parasites hovering overhead—a highly uncharitable thought for someone whose duties sometimes entailed feeding reporters favorable stories. But Englander Center did not need this kind of publicity. If word got out—no, *when* word got out—about the threat, it could have horrible repercussions. People would avoid alternate dispute resolution here for the next ten years. No, less, for the Center would fold long before then.

In any event, she was wrong about Travis, for he wasn't looking up but across the street, toward where a dozen uniformed police exited their marked vehicles. Some headed toward the milling group, obviously charged with crowd control. Others surrounded the SUVs, and Dianna realized they must have something to do with dealing with bombs. That was confirmed as a few men donned what obviously was heavy-duty protective gear.

"Flynn, the bomb—the package that could contain a bomb—was in Dianna's office," Travis continued, his attention back on the people closest to him. "This juggler just happened to be in the right place at the right time. Good citizen that I am, I'm volunteering to show the bomb guys right where it is. You can be most help here if you keep an eye on Dianna for me. You, too, Jeremy and Wally. Just stick close to Dianna while I do what I have to, okay? If she's the target, we've got to protect her. I have to maintain my cover, and I need your help."

"No one needs to—" Dianna began, but Travis kept talking.

"I'll be back soon as I can, but for now, don't let her out of your sight. Keep her in this crowd. You got a cell phone?"

At Jeremy's nod, Travis said, "Give me the number." Wally, always ready with a pocket notebook and pen, jotted it down and handed him the page. "If everything's clear—*when* everything's clear and it's safe to use the phone, I'll call you."

"Fine, Bronson," Jeremy acknowledged, stepping closer to Dianna.

Cal Flynn did not look at all pleased about taking orders from Travis but gave a curt nod.

Emotions warred inside Dianna. Despite his cover as a glib entertainer, Travis Bronson gave orders to everyone who knew about him. Even security specialists. Even her employers.

Even *her*.

She hated that. *Really* hated it.

But what she couldn't fault was that right now, those orders just might save her life.

A WHILE LATER, Dianna stood across Van Nuys Boulevard and down the street, still flanked by her three impromptu bodyguards. They'd tried to get her farther away, but crossing the wide avenue and walking a few blocks had been her only concession.

She glanced at her watch for the zillionth time in the last forty-five minutes and thought about Travis Bronson. Why hadn't he called Jeremy, as he'd promised?

He had gone inside the Center to help the other cops. Had he donned protective gear like the bomb squad? He was trying to maintain the pretense of being a street performer. Would the cops let a supposed civilian risk his life? If not, they should have heard from him by now. Like the rest of the crowd, she had been shooed too far away to see who was entering the building.

What if the place blew up? She would feel responsible if Travis was injured…or worse.

And the idea of that vibrant man never being able to juggle or perform card tricks again. Never issuing orders again. Never *breathing* again…

"If it was going to explode, it would already have happened, wouldn't it?" Wally, who leaned against a metal newspaper dispenser, asked as if reading her thoughts.

But of course they were all thinking about the Center now. What else *could* they think about?

"Maybe," Flynn growled. "Look, guys, I should be there helping."

"You're needed here," Jeremy contradicted with a scowl. He was the only one of her protectors who didn't look wilted from the ordeal or the heat. "You're under orders from the LAPD." His tone made it clear that, as the one who signed the security company's checks, Flynn was under *his* orders, too. "Like Travis said, we have to keep an eye on Dianna."

"You really think that Farley SOB will do something worse right now than set a bomb?" Flynn grumbled. The sheen on his face was even moister now, as the Southern California summer morning grew later and warmer. Dianna had her own suit jacket slung over her arm.

"I don't want to find out." Jeremy put an arm around Dianna's shoulders. She kept herself from pulling away. Even though she'd made it clear that she cared for him like a friend, maybe an uncle, there were times he tested her. She certainly didn't want to hurt his feelings. He'd been so kind. But she simply couldn't get involved with another man now. Brad's death two years earlier still seemed too fresh.

Besides, there were no sparks when it came to Jeremy.

Sparks… Her thoughts again turned to Travis, and she immediately focused them back on here. Now. Reality.

The reality was that Travis had probably gone into a building that might blow up, thanks to one man's vendetta against her husband…and her. She shuddered.

Reality was also Jeremy's arm around her. It tightened at her shaking. "You okay, Dianna?"

She smiled at her boss gently, then took a step as if considering going in the direction he and the others had urged her to go for the last three quarters of an hour—toward a coffee shop several blocks away. She stopped immediately. And gasped.

A man down the street seemed to stare right at her. He was too far away to be sure, yet it could be Farley.

"What's wrong, Ms. Englander?" Flynn asked.

"Right there. It's—" She'd turned briefly to respond to the security man, but when she turned back, the man was gone.

"It's what?"

The crowd had thinned. Most people had wandered off, encouraged by the police, who had cleared a substantial perimeter around Englander Center.

"It's probably my imagination," Dianna said, her heart thudding hard beneath her ribs. "But I think I just saw Farley."

"Where?" Flynn demanded.

She pointed fruitlessly in the general direction.

As the four of them had been swept along with the crowd earlier while crossing the street, Dianna had scanned faces. Farley had to be there. Who else would leave a bomb on her desk?

Of course she hadn't seen him…then. She figured he was too smart to hang around when police were present and she could point him out. After all, his cleverness had kept him from being captured after he killed her husband, despite being on the FBI's Ten Most Wanted list for the cold-blooded murder of a U.S. Representative. He'd even been featured on a national television show that encouraged citizens to report sightings of dangerous fugitives.

At first, as a courtesy, Dianna was scrupulously kept informed about tips, leads and sightings, as if her opinions mattered. But when none resulted in Farley's arrest, she'd asked to be left alone. He could not have been in all the places he had been "seen"—especially since he had so often been around, taunting her.

Not that the federal agents in charge had believed her. Sometimes she'd been treated as having less credibility than the myriad of faceless masses who called—good citizens seeking the monetary award. Her cynicism had come to overpower her fear at seeing Farley—most of the time. She wondered whether that was a good thing.

One thing seemed evident: Farley had to have money to have eluded capture for so long. That's what the authorities told her, for he wasn't like people who lived off the land in wilderness areas to escape apprehension. He'd grown up in urban locales, never served in the military, never even went camping according to family and friends interviewed after he'd fled.

But the reason for his hatred had been poverty—which he had blamed on Brad, who'd promoted redevelopment in areas of urban blight. One such redevelopment had closed down Farley's small business.

Though he'd been paid for the taking of his property, he'd never reopened. He'd blamed Brad for leaving him destitute.

So how had he survived, in a manner that suggested he'd had money to flee?

Dianna's hand again went to her belly. She had been five months pregnant when Farley had used her as bait to bring Brad home one horrible day. He had broken into their house when she had been grocery shopping. When she'd returned, he'd grabbed her, tied her to a kitchen chair, then called Brad. She hadn't intended to say a word, hadn't intended to put her husband in danger. But Farley had made it clear he had no compunction about killing both her and the baby.

Of course Brad had come immediately, unarmed but not without resources. He'd told Farley that the police were outside, demanded that the gun-wielding madman surrender. Farley had tried to make him apologize for his position on urban redevelopment and to promise—on the pain of future peril to his family—that he would stop sponsoring such legislation, but Brad had insisted he would never give in to terrorist threats.

Farley had shot him. And though cops actually had been present, remaining outside at Brad's insistence, Farley had somehow, incredibly, eluded them.

The shock had sent Dianna into premature labor.

"Where'd you say you saw him?" Flynn's harsh tone pierced her thoughts.

"Forget it," she told him. "I was probably mistaken."

"Yeah, just nerves," Flynn agreed. "Even if the guy's around here, he's not about to be so obvious."

Even if? Dianna wanted to cry out in the pain of the

harsh recollection of all she'd lost—her husband. Her baby.

Even her own integrity.

She didn't care whether Cal Flynn believed her. He could join the club.

"You okay, Dianna?" Wally asked, coming closer to stand beside her. "You look awfully pale."

"I'm fine." The lie came as easily as her latest false smile. This was no time to let her thoughts wander like that. .

Time. She looked at her watch again. Another minute had gone by. Another minute in which Farley—if it had been Farley—had escaped again.

Another minute not punctuated by the sound of an explosion.

Another minute in which the bomb disposal unit and the rest of the cops—including Travis—had lived....

Damn! She needed to get away. To think about something other than Farley. She turned abruptly. "Excuse me, guys. I need to—" She was interrupted by the ring of her cell phone, a cheerful tune that didn't match her ominous mood. She reached into her purse and extracted it. The caller ID number on the screen looked vaguely familiar, but she couldn't place it. "Dianna Englander," she answered.

"Travis Bronson," said a deep, strong voice.

"You're okay?" she asked, knowing how silly the question was. He'd called her, not Jeremy. She recalled that she had reluctantly given him her number yesterday. Her knees felt so weak that she lowered herself carefully back into her chair.

"Yeah, I'm fine. Where are you, Dianna? There's something you need to see."

SINCE CIVILIANS WERE being permitted back into the building, Travis decided to wait for Dianna and her shadows there. That way he could hand the evidence right back to one of the Scientific Investigation Division— SID—forensic technicians, so chain of custody wouldn't be a problem.

Assuming there were prints or anything else to tie it to a bad guy. And also assuming they ever apprehended and charged that bad guy so evidence against him could be put to use in a criminal proceeding.

When he'd gone inside the building to show the guys in the Bomb Squad where the bomb was, he'd made a point of bumbling as they'd stuck the protective gear on him, as if he hadn't known what he was doing but was simply obeying their orders. Just in case anyone had been watching. With luck, he'd appeared like a street peddler with a little info, who'd been cooperating with the cops, that was all.

Of course, unlike street peddlers, he always carried, but his weapon remained concealed beneath his pants leg. And it didn't do a hell of a lot of good against a bomb threat.

Now, Travis sat on a soft plaid chair—surprisingly comfortable notwithstanding its designer look and probable price tag—in the brightly lit reception area. Alone. The SID techs were still in Dianna's office. Even though the Van Nuys area, with its many kinds of government offices, was a patchwork of jurisdictions among the city, the county and even the feds, the LAPD stayed in charge of this situation and hadn't needed help.

Where the heck was Dianna? She had said they were only a short distance away, and he'd called ten minutes ago.

"Hi, Travis." The first to enter the office, she ap-

peared out of breath, a little flushed. As if she had hurried all the way back.

His eyes met hers. Her stare was soft and searching.
When she pulled her gaze away, she scanned his body,
as if to make sure he was all in one piece.

Yeah, he sure was. And when she looked him over
like that, *one* of his pieces felt like standing up and sa-
luting.

He turned away quickly, greeting the three guys he'd
nominated as her temporary custodians. They might be
out of shape and stuffy—even the security chief—but
they'd done the job. Dianna, too, remained in one piece.
One lovely, shapely, enticing piece in her form-hugging,
silky green pantsuit…

"Come into my office and tell us what happened,"
she said in a voice that was quiet yet sounded full of
subdued emotion. As if she cared.

Sure, she did care. About the building that bore her
name. No, her *dead husband's* name.

"Nope, your place is still occupied by the investigators." He heard her small gasp of dismay but didn't
respond. If he did, he might want to take her into his
arms and comfort her.

Yeah, some comfort he'd be: an irritated would-be
bodyguard whose interest in her would become obvious
if he held her against him.

Instead, he said, "How about your office, Jeremy?"

The tallest, stuffiest of the mismatched guardian bri-
gade didn't look thrilled, but he acquiesced.

Travis let them precede him down the hall, then followed, carrying a large, sealed plastic evidence bag behind his back.

When they were all seated, he pulled it out.

"What's that?" Wally held out pudgy hands as if to take it.

Travis pulled it back. "No touching. It's a clock."

"We evacuated the whole place for that?" Jeremy sounded irritated. "Was that all that was in the package?"

"If so, then thank heavens," said Dianna. She raised her clear blue eyes quizzically to Travis. A wisp of her blond hair had blown out of place and fluffed up around her ear.

Travis withstood the urge to smooth it down as he nodded. "Pretty much all. There was this, too." He reached into a pocket for the other small evidence bag he'd retained. He handed it to Dianna, who drew in her breath in a sharp whoosh.

It contained a note, written in ink in block letters on a plain white sheet of paper.

"What do you want to bet there'll be no good fingerprints on it?" he asked.

"The way Farley toys with me, he probably wants to be identified." Dianna sounded defeated. Travis didn't like that one bit.

"Maybe. Anyhow, what do you think it means?"

The note read, Time to have a Happy Anniversary, Englander Center.

"This wasn't just a sick joke, was it?" Dianna's voice quivered. "It's a warning. Farley intends to really blow up the Center during the anniversary party."

Chapter Five

"So, do you intend to stay the night?" Dianna despised her waspish tone. But it was either that or let her inner trembling show, and she would choose nasty over vulnerable any day.

Especially where Lt. Travis Bronson was concerned.

And particularly since the idea of the much-too-sexy undercover cop staying the night at her home was spraying ignited flares up and down her psyche.

"Do you want me to?" he countered. His grin was slow, sensuous and altogether too tempting.

"No," she replied quickly. "I just want to be left alone."

The problem was, she wasn't sure she *did* want to be left alone. Not after today's scare. Not after everything else that scratched her nerve endings until they were frayed enough to scream.

Travis and she stood in the high-ceilinged entry of her Tudor-style home. On two sides were halls that led to the spacious living and entertaining areas of the first floor, and straight ahead was the sweeping stairway to the floor above. Travis scanned the place as if memorizing it, as she'd seen him do with each new location he visited with her.

He hadn't changed clothes, so the same worn blue jeans hugged his slim hips. She'd noticed—oh, yes, she'd noticed—that his maroon T-shirt with the pushcart logo was damp with perspiration earlier, after he removed the protective gear he admitted to wearing. It was dry now but still outlined every hard muscle of his chest, particularly as he pivoted to look over her home.

Who was he? Had he grown up in L.A.? Was he married?

Why did she want to know?

"Have you been a police officer long?" she asked.

"About six years."

"And before that?"

He scowled, apparently not happy with her questions. "College, and before that the Army."

"Are you originally from—"

"If you're sure you want me to go," he interrupted, "I'll leave."

She blinked in the bright light from the polished brass fixture above them. Surely she hadn't heard right. This domineering, overly protective man was suggesting that she stay by herself after today's threat? Was it because she'd dared to ask questions? He knew *her* background. He'd done his homework.

"Fine, go ahead," she said, then cleared her throat, angry at her hoarseness.

"But you'll still be under surveillance all night. Like you were last night." He turned to look at her again, the brilliance of his deep blue eyes daring her to challenge him.

And of course she did. Or at least she started to. "What do you mean, surveillance? I told you I wanted—"

"What you want is to survive, isn't it?" He crossed his sinewy, hair-dusted arms over his chest.

"Yes." The word escaped before she had time to consider a measured response. But what difference did it make? The answer would be the same, no matter how she said it.

"Well, then, that's something we can agree on."

"A first," she acknowledged.

His ironic smile lifted a corner of his wide, masculine mouth. One light brown eyebrow arched. "No need to pay me to agree with you."

"What—" She began, as his hand reached out and gently moved aside her hair. She all but shuddered at the touch that felt much too intimate as it skimmed her ear. She watched his eyes darken in apparent sensual awareness. "Travis, I—"

"Here." His voice was as raspy as hers was earlier. With a flourish, he waved a quarter that he appeared to have removed from behind her ear.

She couldn't help smiling at the errant magician as she reached for the coin. It was warm from the heat of his fingers. She wondered for a moment, as she looked into his eyes, just what heat those magical fingers might generate along skin at more erogenous parts of her body.

"I don't suppose you do that with hundred-dollar bills," she said quickly, crossing her arms in protective withdrawal.

He obviously noticed the gesture, for his gaze was instantly drawn down to her folded arms. At first. She realized after a moment he was looking beyond them. To her curves, beneath her blouse. Damn. The magician had managed to warm her without even touching her this time.

"I can work any kind of magic you want," he said

huskily, his smoky blue eyes rising to captivate hers once more.

"Then I want to be left alone," she repeated stubbornly. No double entendres there. But she was lying even more this time. She took a step back for emphasis. "Besides, how can you keep up your cover, pretend to be a street entertainer, and come to my home like this?"

"You're attracted to me, of course." His tone was glib, his eyes smiling. He knew he was lying. Wasn't he? "Slumming a little, though you're just leading me on. I'm trying to convince you to hire me to put together entertainers for your anniversary fund-raiser, so I'm playing along. We'll do a dialogue or two in public to that effect, so my cover won't be breached."

"Right. I'm slumming." She scowled. "But anyone who knows me realizes I don't even…" She tapered off. It wasn't his business that she didn't date. Didn't have a social life at all. Didn't want one.

"Besides, since it's what you want, tonight you'll be alone in your house," he said brusquely, all cop again, his cover notwithstanding. "But I'll have a team outside watching to make sure there's no activity here."

"Fine. Go home to your wife. Maybe she won't mind your telling her what to do." Dianna could have kicked herself for saying that. She could simply have asked him.

And maybe he'd have answered.

"I'm not married." He sounded amused. "Now, if you hear anything out of the ordinary tonight, call me. I'll be home all by myself. Got it?"

No! she wanted to shout. As he turned toward the door, she yearned to beg for him to stay. To protect her.

To touch her…

"Got it," she managed to say.

BACK IN HIS CAR, Travis made calls to get a surveillance team ready. Then he sat back, tuned into some sultry jazz on a local station, turned it low, and waited for his backup.

He'd parked on the street after following Dianna home when she'd finished a full day of work. Amazing lady. After that sick joke, after possibly even spotting that SOB Farley again, she'd apparently hunkered right down and done her job.

Yeah, and her diligence wasn't the only thing he found amazing about her. Her hair had been every bit as silky to the touch as he'd imagined. And then there was the way her lush mouth quivered a little, then took on a determined set as she defied him. Defied the world.

More than once, he'd wanted to lay his own hungry lips right on that very appealing mouth…

Come on, Bronson, he taunted himself. *You're steaming the damn car windows all by yourself.*

She'd wanted to know if he was married. Hell, he'd learned before he was even Julie Alberts' age, when his folks died, that getting close to anyone was a mistake. And the one time he'd tried it, he'd found out just how much of a mistake. Cassi had died, thanks to him.

He glanced out the misty windows, taking in all directions to make sure nothing seemed amiss on the narrow, twisting street in the hills. It was late December and dark out, so even as early as 8:30 p.m. he had to rely on streetlights and security lights gleaming from private property for illumination. Palm trees and eucalyptus towered above the lightposts. Many homeowners here in the hills of the San Fernando Valley kept their places private by building block walls or growing tall hedges, so there weren't a lot of homes to scrutinize.

Cars—that was a different matter. Angelenos loved

their wheels. Most households had more vehicles than spots in their garages or on their steep driveways. People showed how important they thought they were by the cost of their transportation.

Travis had no argument with his Jeep. Though it was eight years old, it was reliable.

His cover for being there? Right now, he was a stalker of sorts. The juggler had a crush on his would-be employer. Any fool who got a look at Dianna would understand that.

He sat up and watched when he heard a sweet, grumbling engine. A Jag drove by. The driver looked balding, middle-aged and damn proud of his place in the world. Travis stroked his vehicle's dash to reassure the aging hunk of horsepower. Not all wheels could be Jags.

He looked back outside. His scrutiny ended where he'd last seen the woman who set his teeth—and other hard body parts—on edge. Nice house. It didn't hide behind foliage, though maybe it should, for security. He studied it, squinting in the meandering row of lights illuminating the path up the lawn.

Its facade was attractive. Looked European, half-timbered along the second story. It rambled a bit on a rambling lot, must have cost big bucks up here where the view doubled the price.

Maybe one day he'd bite the bullet and put a down payment on something like it, and—

Who the hell was he trying to kid? Yeah, it was a nice house, inside and out. Way out of his class. Just like the lady who lived there was way beyond his dreams.

"Where the hell are you, Perez?" he muttered, speaking of the team member who was supposed to take his place.

He was ready to leave, the sooner the better.

SITTING IN HER downstairs den at the front of the house, Dianna didn't let herself look out the blinds. She figured Travis was gone, but he'd left someone watching her house. Watching over her. That, she supposed, was good. But she was still kicking herself for not asking him to stay. To sleep in a guest room, of course, but at least that way she'd be able to sleep, knowing Travis was there to make sure she was all right.

She made a self-mocking sound. Right. As if her wayward body would have allowed her to sleep, with the sexy cop only a wall or two away. Not that she considered herself a seductress, but she'd surely have had the urge to go knock on his door. Throw herself at him.

After all, his *cover* was that she was attracted to him....

"Good thing you're there and I'm here," she muttered to the absent Travis, wherever his "there" might be right then.

She sat back on the couch and pressed the remote button to turn on her television. Mistake, for the channel she'd put on ran local news for hours, starting early

And there, before her very eyes, was that morning's evacuation of Englander Center.

"Oh, no," she cried. But what had she expected?

Fortunately, the segment was short. She sat up straighter when the on-the-spot reporter shoved a microphone in Wally Sellers's face, in front of one of several bail-bond shops along Van Nuys Boulevard. When had he agreed to a media interview, and why hadn't he told her? *She* was the Center's media contact.

"It was an unfortunate situation," Wally said into the microphone. Dianna had always heard that being on camera added ten pounds to a person's girth, which appeared true with chubby Wally. His suit jacket bulged, and his extra chins pleated further as he lowered his head to talk into the sound equipment. "But no harm was done," he continued. "Englander Center is fine, and so is the wonderful work we do to help people resolve their problems. Your viewers are welcome to come to our anniversary celebration next week to see for themselves."

Dianna had to grin despite her concern. Wally was making the proverbial lemonade out of a lemon, turning what he called an "unfortunate situation" into a promotion for the Center. *Good move, Wally,* she thought.

But her grin faded as she recalled her conversation with Travis about the so-called joke bomb, the note—and the Center's anniversary celebration.

Maybe Wally had just invited the entire television viewing audience to celebrate by being blown up along with Englander Center, courtesy of Glen Farley.

TRAVIS WHEELED THE BRIGHT yellow, large-wheeled miniature pushcart down the hall of the sixth floor at Englander Center—the same floor that had been the focus of yesterday's excitement.

He pushed open the door of the offices of A-S Development—Alberts and Sellers, Jeremy and Wally. The developers and managers of the building. And employers of Dianna Englander.

"Hi," he said to Beth, the attractive receptionist who stood at the indoor hallway. "Up for coffee and doughnuts this morning?" He hadn't revealed his real job to her and hoped no one else had either—or to anyone else.

"Yes to coffee, no to doughnuts." Beth's laugh was

melodic, her bright smile contagious as she drew nearer.
"Though I'm tempted."

"Let me coax you to give in to temptation." He gave
a teasing leer, which caused her to laugh again.

Unlike the more somberly-clad professional types
around here, she was dressed in a sweater of bright ma-
genta over a dark skirt. Looked good on her. He'd
dressed for the occasion, too. No T-shirt today, but a
blue denim work shirt.

"The answer is no!" A shrill male voice hurtled from
somewhere inside the offices. "We're not going to cancel."

Sharing a glance with Beth, Travis tried to hear the
more muted response, with no success. Sounded like
Wally, he thought, but it could have been a rattled Jeremy.

"Someone needs a cup of coffee." He wheeled the
cart over the plush carpet toward the office's inner sanc-
tum.

"I don't think that's a good idea," Beth protested.

But Travis maneuvered around her. He guessed that
the office from which the voice had issued was the second one. He knocked but didn't wait for an answer before pushing the door open. "Breakfast!" he called.

The office was Wally's, or at least he was the one
standing stiffly behind the desk. His face was so scarlet
that Travis wondered if he had burst a blood vessel.

Facing him, standing on his Berber rug, were an
equally angry Jeremy, and Dianna, who looked pale in
her blue suit.

Travis resisted the urge to grab her and squeeze,
though she looked like she could use a hug. And he
would have enjoyed being on the other end of that embrace.

But not then. And not at all, if he was smart. Physical closeness could lead to mental closeness. He was already more attracted to her than was good for him. Or her.

He knew she'd not been bothered last night by prowlers or prank calls. With her consent, her phone was monitored, and he'd checked with his guys who'd been on duty. Things had been quiet, including on the way here this morning, for she'd been under protective surveillance then as well.

But things around her were not quiet now.

"You guys hungry?" He grinned into the angry glowers of the two men. He didn't give them time to answer before gently closing the door in Beth's scowling face. "So, what's up?"

"Not your concern, Bronson." Jeremy Alberts seemed to force himself to relax, if someone who always looked like he had a stick up his butt could ever loosen up. He sat in one of the mismatched chairs facing his partner's desk and glared at Wally.

Wally sat down, too. "It's just company business, Lt. Bronson," he said. "Nothing you need to be concerned about."

"Is that right, Dianna?" he asked. She had remained standing, and her soft blue eyes had widened with what Travis would guess was exasperation. Maybe even a hint of incredulity.

"We need a professional's opinion," she said, only obliquely addressing his question. "I suggested that we not make a big deal about the Center's first anniversary celebration next week. If we cancel the fund-raiser and ceremony—"

"Then that damned Farley will have won!" Wally exploded. "And it's not like that bomb threat was real. In fact, it put us in the news. Just think of the turnout we'll have, all the extra people we can introduce to the good work we do here.''

''And all the extra people we'll put in danger,'' Dianna said, her expression fragile and bruised, as if she took the blame for hurting every single one of them.

Her vulnerability had the power of a serrated knife as it slashed Travis in the gut. He held on to the mini-pushcart to keep from getting closer to her.

''My opinion,'' Jeremy said before Travis could offer his own, ''is that we could postpone the celebration or cancel it, but why bother? If Farley wants to create chaos here, he'll find a way, whether on the actual one-year anniversary or some other time. Don't you agree, Lieutenant?''

Travis looked again at Dianna for her reaction. Damn. The expression on her face was pleading. She undoubtedly hoped he would demand that they cancel the event. Maybe even shut down the building for the next month.

But what she really wanted was for him to find Farley.

He wanted to find Farley, too. Lock him up, cast him so deep into the legal system that he'd never see daylight again.

If Travis weren't a cop, sworn to uphold the law, he'd even consider personally exterminating the vermin, to save the taxpayers' money. But law enforcement all over the country hadn't caught the guy. Travis wanted to be the one. Hell, he *intended* to be the one. But not at the expense of other lives.

Especially Dianna's.

Yet Jeremy Alberts had a point. What was one day among thirty-one this month, three hundred sixty-five this year? Farley would make whatever damned statement he wanted, whenever he chose. It was better to act as if he didn't scare anyone. Maybe that would make him angry. And anger begot carelessness.

And so, ignoring the plea in Dianna's gorgeous, sad, fearful eyes, he poured a cup of rich-smelling black coffee, handed it to her and said, "I'm with Jeremy. Let's toast the Englander Center's birthday celebration."

Chapter Six

Dianna paced her office. Anger— she wasn't about to admit even to herself that it was fear, too— made her want to hurl something against the wall. Better yet, against Travis.

If he'd insisted, half an hour earlier, on postponing the celebration, her stubborn bosses would have listened. He was, after all, authoritative. A cop.

Even if he hid that fact behind the persona of a juggling magician.

A too-sexy juggling magician, whose solid, sensual physique, as he performed his engaging tricks, made Dianna feel like pulling pranks of her own.

Like last night. Maybe if she'd played her own cards right, he'd have stayed in her house, and—

And they'd have spent the time rehashing the bomb scare. Platonic stuff. Which would have been one heck of a lot better than yearning after the hunk who kept telling her what to do.

Who was permitting the birthday celebration despite her disapproval…

Enough. She couldn't hang out here all day pouting like a child who hadn't gotten her own way.

Besides, she couldn't help the niggling thought that

going forward *was* the right thing. It would shove Farley's threats back in his vicious, murderous face. The face only she had seen. Over and over, from the day he killed Brad, and intermittently for months afterward.

With a noise of combined anxiety and exasperation, she slung over her shoulder the jacket to the deceptively cheerful royal-blue suit she'd donned that day, grabbed her purse from a drawer and fled her office.

"I'm going downstairs," she told Beth, who looked up from her computer in the reception area. "Bill Hultman of Legal Eats left a message that he wanted to talk to me."

Legal Eats, a small restaurant, was one of three retail establishments on the Center's first floor. The others were a bank and a convenience store. Plus, there was a large community room. All were intended to promote good relations between Englander Center and people frequenting the Van Nuys civic area.

Normally, Dianna would return Bill's call before heading to see him, but she needed to get out of her office. To concentrate on something besides Farley and the way he toyed with her.

And on something besides Travis…

"Have you talked to the police today?" Beth asked, startling Dianna.

"Yes…er, no." She had talked to Travis, of course, but Beth didn't know he was a cop. The receptionist had been with A-S Development since Englander Center had opened, but Travis had been blunt, as usual, about warning Dianna that *she* wasn't to tell anyone who he really was. *He* would share that information when he found it wise or expedient. Meantime, *she* had to pretend to flirt with him.

Pretend?

"Why do you ask about the cops?" she continued to cover her near-blunder.

"I wondered if they know more about yesterday's bomb scare. How did you keep so cool about a ticking package on your desk?"

Dianna's mind immediately lurched into suspicion. "How did you know about that?"

The information released to the media, despite Wally's over-eager interview, hadn't been specific about the nature of the suspected bomb. According to Travis, that would ensure, if they heard from the usual crazies who confessed to everything from jaywalking to terrorism, that the cops could cull the crank calls from people who might have genuine information.

Beth hadn't been on the need-to-know list.

Beth's large, dark eyes grew somber with hurt. "Wally told me." She stood, crossing her arms. Beneath the curve of her wavy black hair, the tiny filigree balls dangling from her ears vibrated, indicating her quivering tension. "How did you think I knew?" she asked defensively. "Because I put it there? Why would I?" Despite the defiance in the jut of her full, pouting lips, Dianna saw hurt there, too.

"Of course not," she said quickly. Since she'd spotted Farley in the crowd, she knew who'd planted the bomb—as if she'd had any doubt even before. It wasn't a matter of opportunity. Dianna wouldn't be surprised if a terrorist toting an AK-47 could get into the building past Cal Flynn's shaky security detail, screening machines notwithstanding. Piece of cake for the elusive Farley, who'd gotten away with murder—several times.

Brad's murder...

"Sorry, Beth," Dianna said. "I didn't mean to imply

anything. It's just that I didn't really keep my cool after that scare.''

''Guess not.'' Beth didn't sound mollified as she turned back to her keyboard.

Did she protest too much? After all, how easy would it have been for her to come in with a package containing a ticking clock and put in on Dianna's desk?

Pretty darned easy, if Beth had a reason.

But Dianna couldn't think of any. No, it was Glen Farley. He was out there somewhere, waiting for her....

''See you later,'' she said to Beth, then hurriedly fled the office. Too bad she couldn't leave her disturbing thoughts behind so easily.

WHY WAS TRAVIS THERE? Dianna thought five minutes later as she entered Legal Eats.

In contrast with the Center's resplendent lobby, the restaurant was small, a glorified lunchroom where people who were part of the building's legal system and their clients, the litigants, could grab coffee and a snack while on breaks.

Travis ostensibly worked on an outside pushcart that brimmed with food and drinks. He had no business sitting at one of the small glass-topped tables nursing a cup of coffee while reading the paper.

It was almost as if he knew she'd be there.

That impression was bolstered by the fact that he immediately looked up and winked, as if he'd expected her arrival at that precise moment. Which annoyed Dianna all the more.

No matter how that slow, suggestive wink had sent shivers of sexual awareness up her back.

It's his cover, she reminded herself. She ignored the feeling, but she couldn't ignore Travis—even as she realized the most obvious reason for his being here. She'd seen no one keeping an eye on her since she'd arrived at work. Her unwanted bodyguard must be on duty once more.

Irritation warred with relief. For the moment, at least, she was safe. Maybe.

She shot Travis a nod of greeting, then headed for the counter.

The restaurant was nearly empty. Only one table beside Travis's was occupied. The people there appeared to be an attorney and client, discussing a case.

Bill Hultman, owner of Legal Eats, stood behind the counter facing three customers seated there. Out of habit these days, Dianna looked them over. One was female. The others looked familiar, people who worked in the building.

None was Farley.

Bill, in his forties, was a former lawyer himself who'd had a heart attack and jogged out of that rat race into a different kind with stresses of its own. His long, dour face was perpetually ruddy, which could indicate high blood pressure. Dianna, who'd helped to negotiate his lease, had wanted more than once to talk him into slowing down.

He looked up as she approached, and his expression was not welcoming. Drat. A good reason to have called first: she'd have come armed with knowledge of what he wanted to discuss.

"How's a business supposed to survive, Dianna," he demanded with no preamble, "with all this nasty stuff going on?"

"I'm sorry, Bill," she soothed, "but fortunately bomb scares don't happen every day." She hoped. And she hoped even more fervently that the next time wouldn't be a bomb *blast* instead of merely a scare.

She felt Travis's attention bore into her back. She'd no doubt he was taking in this conversation, while appearing to be engrossed in his newspaper.

"I don't just mean bomb scares!" The explosion in the restaurant at that moment came from its owner. "That's one thing, but then there are those damned push-cart peddlers. I know you can't do anything about their being outside, cutting into my business with their stupid tricks that draw customers, but I've seen them wheeling food upstairs, right inside this building. That you can control. And as your tenant, I demand that you put a stop to it."

"Er—I'll see what I can do," Dianna dissembled. But since Travis's pushcart venture was a means of scrutinizing the building and its occupants, she was unlikely to end it. Or want to. Didn't Bill recognize his current customer Travis from the cart? Probably. His vituperative outpouring was likely aimed at the man he considered his competition, who just happened to be patronizing his restaurant. "I think there's an agreement between my bosses and the vendor," she continued. That was more or less true.

"I don't care about any other damned agreements!" Bill shouted. "I'm losing so much business that maybe a bomb wouldn't be such a bad idea after all. It might be the only way to get out of your damned lease." And then, as if he heard what he'd said, he muttered, "I didn't mean that."

But Dianna wondered...

Of course these days she wondered about everyone's motivations. Farley was most likely acting on his own, yet there was all the speculation about whether he'd had help getting away in the first place, and second, third and more. He'd eluded the finest law enforcement agen cies in the country, over and over.

But it was unlikely that this edgy former lawyer pleading poverty would have been much assistance.

"Why don't you compete with the carts?" Dianna said, hoping to placate the angry entrepreneur. "Or promote your full breakfasts. Or cut prices on the things you carry that are the same as what's on the carts."

"Yeah. Maybe." He seemed to consider what she said, even as the customers at the counter tossed out suggestions of their own: karaoke to compete with the juggling. Drawings for a free lunch for people who deposited business cards in a box. Bill calmed considerably, and Dianna surreptitiously sighed in relief.

To mollify him further, she said, "Know what? I'm hungry. I need breakfast. And coffee. Definitely coffee." She ordered her food, accepted a full cup from him, then went to sit at a vacant table.

She wasn't alone long. Travis joined her. That day, he wore a blue denim shirt with sleeves rolled up to reveal his lean, hair-sprinkled forearms, and jeans a few shades darker. She'd noticed before in Wally's office. She was noticing way too much what this man wore.

Even as she couldn't help speculating how he would look with no clothes on at all…

She'd been a widow too long. Her carnal urges were running amok. When all this was over, she'd have to find a nice, simple, straightforward lover. One with no strings attached.

No demands made, no orders given.

As if that were something she could do…

"I don't know if you should sit there," she said to

Travis even as he sat down. "Bill might interpret it as my associating with his enemy."

"The way I see it, he considers everyone his enemy." Travis set his half-empty cup on the table. Dianna noticed that he took his coffee black. "A good reason to keep tabs on *him*. If he makes good on any of his threats, we'll catch him in the act."

Dianna realized she wasn't the only one who suspected everyone of affiliating with Farley. That might result from *her* paranoia, but it was part of Travis's job.

"So," he continued, "you still mad at me after this morning?" His grin seemed designed to pick a fight.

He wouldn't get his way. "No. I wasn't mad then, either. I think going forward with the celebration is ill-advised, but I definitely don't want Farley to think he's won."

"Good girl." There was frank admiration in his deep blue eyes, and she felt herself flush. "And as long as you listen to me, I'll be sure you're safe."

Dianna's back stiffened as fast as if he'd pushed her hard against a wall. In a way, he had. "And you're promising that if I obey your every command, Farley won't get to me? Ever?"

"Yeah." But despite the fierceness that set his jaw, Dianna thought she saw just a hint of doubt pierce his hard expression. If so, it was so fleeting that she was sure she'd imagined it.

In any event, she wasn't about to simply buckle under to his insistence on obedience. "So that means you're better than the Washington D.C. police, the FBI and the Secret Service, too. There'd been threats against my husband Brad, and none of them were able to keep Farley from killing him." *Or my baby*... She took a deep breath and continued before Travis could respond. "They couldn't find him, either, after he'd committed murder. Then there are the others who've not been able to keep him from destroying buildings in redevelopment areas. Not even here in Los Angeles. And sometimes people have died.''

"Yeah, maybe I'm better than them all. And you will be fine, Ms. Englander, as long as you—'' His words, uttered in a clipped monotone, were interrupted by Bill Hultman's slinging a plate of scrambled eggs and bacon in front of her.

"Eat up,'' Bill said. "This stuff tastes good, and it's served right here, in these delightful surroundings.'' He glared at Travis. "Most of all, it won't kill you. 'Cause you can bet on the fact that if things don't change around here fast, and for the better, someone's going to pay.''

OKAY, SO HE liked to play with fire. What else was new? Travis thought as he stood silently in the elevator with a steaming Dianna and a couple of lawyers talking about the weather. As if winter weather in L.A. was worth wasting any words on: cool, and not enough rain this year. As usual.

He'd caught Dianna's furious glare a couple of minutes earlier when he'd gotten right into the face of the threatening restaurant jockey and grinned, told the nasty SOB that he'd have a special on glazed doughnuts the next day on the little cart he took around inside the building. Did Hultman want one?

What Hultman obviously wanted was to lay one right on Travis's chin. But Travis made it clear he'd frown on such a thing. And Hultman had been the one to back down.

And soon as Travis left the restaurant, trailing after the obviously riled Dianna, he'd called on his cell phone and had a background check started on the pig-iron chef of Englander Center. He hoped he'd find a record a mile long on the guy. That'd give Travis even more impetus to goad him.

If there were any possible ties to Farley... Well, the guy would be lucky if he'd have any food to eat again outside prison, let alone any to sell to the trusting public.

So far, though, his investigators were batting zero. The car license number Dianna had seen a couple days earlier yielded nothing useful. And the calls to her house had been placed from pay phones right here in Van Nuys.

Dianna wasn't talking to Travis now. He didn't blame her, yet the silent treatment created an unfamiliar emptiness inside him. He was used to silence. Being alone.

They reached the floor where her office was, and she stomped out of the elevator. He followed, ignoring the interested stares of the couple of suits who'd accompanied them. *Get back to your discussion of the palm trees, guys.*

He followed Dianna down the hall, the sway of her hips beneath her blue skirt, as her irritation played out in her forceful pace, making him nearly giddy with a need to stroke them. Hold them. Hold *her.*

But when she entered the reception area and tried to close the door on him, he returned to reality.

It was time she did, too.

His reality was that she was under his protection. He wasn't going to let anything happen to her, whether she liked it or not.

Never again would he fail to protect someone he was assigned to watch. And that also meant staying detached. She was a subject, not a sex object. Period.

Remember that, he silently reminded his aching libido.

"So, Ms. Englander," he said aloud. "We need to talk about what you're going to need for me to bring this afternoon for your meeting."

"What—?" Her blistering blue eyes blazed, but she caught herself, casting a quick sidelong glance behind her, where the pretty receptionist was taking in every word. "Oh, of course. Please come into my office."

He didn't need to be asked twice. But though he'd intended to lay down the law as to how she'd cooperate with him, she was the one to round on him first, soon as she'd reached her side of her desk. "What was all that about?"

"What was *what* about?"

"The way you threatened Bill Hultman."

Travis narrowed his eyes but managed to keep his voice level. "Way I saw it, he threatened me. Not to mention *you*. That made me a touch cranky, so I figured I'd let him know, not keep my emotions to myself. Isn't that what women like to say?"

The glare she shot at him made it clear that she, at least, was one woman who didn't keep her emotions to herself. But she sank slowly onto her desk chair.

He didn't much like the idea of being a nasty son of a bitch toward her, but he had to get his point across while he had her attention. "Look, Dianna. I'm sorry if you prefer subtlety, but that's not the way I work. Someone's in my face, I deal with it. Someone's in the face of a person I'm keeping watch over, that's even worse, and I don't let it happen."

"I appreciate that," she said wearily. "And I have to admit I'm sick of worrying."

"Let me take care of that."

The slow, tired smile that illuminated her lovely face

tugged at something inside him in the vicinity of where his heart would be, if he had one. "Thanks."

Good. Now he had her attention, this was the time to make his point. "But you have to help. And that means cooperating with me."

"How?" Her smile transmogrified into wariness.

"You need to keep me informed every time you move so I can make sure Farley's not harassing you. Like this morning. You left your office without telling me. I need to know when you go so if I can't keep an eye on you, I'll put someone else on it."

"You found me fast enough." She didn't sound pleased.

"Just luck. I happened to call a second after you left, and that nice young lady Beth wasn't hard to convince that I had to find you to discuss a catering job, fast. She told me where you'd gone."

"A catering job from a vendor's pushcart?"

"You just backed me up a minute ago."

She nodded slowly. "I guess I did. But I really don't like the idea of my whole life becoming a game of 'Mother May I.' Being accountable to anyone isn't... Well, it's not something I like. Or do well."

Had her dear, departed husband, the worthy U.S. Representative Brad Englander, accepted that? Maybe. But maybe her strong reaction to Travis was because she'd been given little choice during her marriage to the powerful politician.

"I figured that," Travis responded. "But for now, till I've got Farley in my sights, I'm asking you to do that one little thing for me. Okay?"

Her prolonged hesitation made it clear how much she wanted to say no. But eventually, she nodded. "Okay.

As long as it makes sense, I'll let you know where I'm going.''

''It *always* makes sense,'' he said.

"DIANNA, I THINK you'd better take this call.'' Beth's voice sounded frantic. ''I've tried to find Jeremy, but he must have turned his cell phone off.''

''Sure,'' Dianna said. ''But who—'' She realized immediately that Beth had cut her off to go back to the caller. Leaning forward on her desk, Dianna held the receiver close to her ear, prepared to hear another complaint about something that had gone wrong in the building.

Not another bomb scare, she prayed. Or another call from Bill Hultman, with something to add to his list of grumbles from an hour earlier.

It turned out less scary than a bomb threat, but a whole lot worse than a continuation of Bill's tirade. ''Ms. Englander, this is Pearl Kinch, the principal of Beverly Vista Middle School. I understand you are Julie Alberts' aunt.'' Which was true by closeness to the family, if not by blood relationship. ''She's gotten into trouble here today, and we need someone to come take her home immediately.''

THE ELEVATOR WAS filled when it reached the sixth floor on the way downstairs, but Dianna shoehorned her way onto it. She found herself sandwiched between two families with small children—five youngsters between them. Two were crying, and the parents were obviously at wits' end trying to keep them under control.

''I'm so sorry,'' one harried mother said after the little girl in her arms stiffened and one leg brushed Dianna's arm.

"That's all right. Were they with you in one of the offices upstairs?"

"Yes, and the mediator kept us waiting because her last case ran over. I'd have gotten a sitter, but I can't afford one every time we come here, and—"

"I understand," Dianna assured the woman. That was exactly why she intended to build her child-care center downstairs. Soon.

The elevator reached the ground floor, and as everyone poured out, Dianna realized how grateful she'd been for the small distraction. That Mrs. Kinch refused to tell exactly what was wrong with Julie. She'd sounded angry, cold and spiteful.

Poor Julie. Dianna had to go rescue her. Stick up for her, no matter what it was, for she needed someone in her corner.

As she headed through the lobby for the separate elevator to the parking lot, she saw security chief Cal Flynn using a wand to check for metal carried by an obviously exasperated man in a dark suit, most likely an attorney.

But had Farley sneaked in by pretending to belong here, wearing a suit…?

Oh, lord. Farley. His wretched name reminded her of Travis, and her quasi-promise that morning to keep him closely informed of her whereabouts.

To let him accompany her.

The idea of having his protection did feel comforting, but surely there was no reason for him to leave whatever he was doing that day to scurry off with her to Julie's school. Still, she'd said she'd let him know.

She glanced outside. His pushcart was there, and so was the man who ran it, Manny.

But Travis wasn't.

And Dianna hated the idea of leaving Julie in the formidable Mrs. Kinch's bad graces any longer than necessary.

She pulled Travis's cell phone number from her purse and used her own to call him. Quickly, she explained the situation.

"Wait there," he demanded, "in the lobby. I'm at the Van Nuys police station but I'll be there in five minutes to go with you."

"That's not necessary."

"We've discussed this, Dianna." His tone was chilly and challenging. "Wait for me."

"Tell you what," she said. Compromise was the key here. After all, her job was renting out facilities in which negotiations and compromises were the stuff of everyday life.

"I'll go get my car and pick you up in front of the building, on Van Nuys Boulevard."

"Dianna—" His voice grated from between clenched teeth. She didn't have to see him to know that, by its sound.

"Five minutes," she said.

She got onto the elevator and pushed the button for the second floor, where she'd parked that morning in her reserved spot.

When the door opened, she quickly headed toward her sports car, her key out so she could unlock it remotely.

As she reached for the door, someone grabbed her from behind. An arm went around her neck, choking her. Tighter.

Tighter.

Chapter Seven

Frightened at the increasingly constricting pressure at her throat, Dianna flailed out.

They were in a public garage. Where were all the people? Why was she alone?

Better that she was alone. No one else would get hurt. Besides her.

The pressure continued to tighten. A leg wrapped around one of hers, so that if she tried to run, she would trip.

She couldn't move.

Could hardly breathe…

"So you're still here, Mrs. Englander? Dianna?" said a voice that haunted her nightmares. She'd heard it first on the night Farley had taken her prisoner to lure Brad to his death. "Not good at heeding warnings, are you?"

"What do you wa—?" Her throat ached from the pressure, and she couldn't finish.

The laugh was a horrifying cackle. "What do I want? That's rich. No one asked me before, when your dear departed husband ruined my business. Ruined *me*. But know what? I'm enjoying my little game now. Maybe I should thank Brad. In fact, I am thanking him by sending him a present, because very soon his beloved wife is going to join him.'' His conversational tone turned to a menacing roar. "In hell!''

She should have listened to Travis, Dianna thought fleetingly. In a moment, she would lose consciousness, and he'd have the pleasure of thinking, *I told you so.* Only he wouldn't be able to direct it at her.

She'd be dead.

No! She wouldn't give Farley the satisfaction. He'd taken from her all she'd held dear. Her husband. Her baby.

No more.

Farley wasn't a tall man, but he was larger than she. She was gripped tightly, her head fixed against his disgustingly damp chest. He smelled rank, as if his nerves made him sweat. Good.

She would make him sweat even more.

Gasping for air, she used the only two weapons she could think of: surprise, and the key she held in her hand. She shrieked, kicked backward with the leg that wasn't fettered by him. The pressure at her neck tightened even further, but she used the leverage of her body to pull Farley off balance.

At the same time, she twisted, gagging at the yank at her neck, but in a moment she faced him. Saw his startled, hateful face. A long face, pouchy and lined. He needed a shave. Gray hair bristled among darker brown that matched damp waves clinging to a high forehead.

And then there were his eyes. Brown. Huge. Smug. Glittering with laughter.

Insane.

He still held her arm. His grip tightened. Dianna raised her hand and slammed the key against Farley's fleshy cheek, just below his right eye, and shoved hard even as she sliced downward.

He screamed and released her.

"Dianna!" called a hollow voice in the distance, from the stairwell.

Travis? Was he coming to help her?

Just in case, she grabbed at Farley, trying to hang onto him as he'd held her.

But she was weakened from their struggle, and he was stronger. He was a man.

A man with strength born of madness.

He wrested away. Blood poured from the deep gouge in his face, and the malevolent glare he trained on her made her cry out. "Travis!" she yelled, grabbing toward Farley again.

Too late. He jumped into a car and the engine roared to life.

The smell of exhaust surrounded Dianna as Farley drove maniacally down the ramp, screeching between the other cars, before he was out of sight.

Gone.

She was safe.

She didn't recall falling to her knees, but that was where she was, gasping, when Travis emerged from the stairwell.

"Dianna!" In a moment, he was by her side. "What happened? You're bleeding!"

Only then did she notice the blood on the hand that still held the key. Disgusted, horrified, she let the small piece of metal drop. It pinged on the concrete floor.

"I'm all right," she managed, her throat aching. "I got free. I scratched Farley's face."

"Farley? He was here?"

She nodded.

"How the hell did he get past the security guards downstairs?" Travis demanded. "Anyone worth his damn job should be able to recognize him from the composite sketches that have been circulated.''

Dianna could only shrug. ''He's always been elusive,'' she rasped.

But Travis wasn't done with his tirade. ''And why aren't there security cameras in this place?''

Dianna had no answer. Didn't care about the answer, for the reality of what had happened was sinking in.

''He wanted to kill me.'' Tears welled in her eyes. She felt as if she were going to throw up.

''But you got him instead?''

Before she could respond, she was lifted to her feet, but the wobbliness of her legs didn't matter, for Travis pulled her firmly against his chest.

This time, she didn't mind being held tightly by a man. This time, it was comforting.

This time, it was Travis.

''You're okay?'' he murmured softly into her hair. ''That's what's really important here.''

''Yes, I'm okay.'' Her voice was little more than a whisper. ''Sort of.''

''He didn't hurt you?''

''He choked me. Why now? He could have killed me before, if he'd wanted to. Why— ''

She gave a small cry of protest as Travis pulled back to inspect her. Very gently, his fingers touched her throat. She winced, for even the slight contact made her aware of her bruising. ''Damn him.'' The steely look on Travis's face made it clear he meant it literally. To him, Farley was damned.

Dianna had the feeling that Travis would risk himself, his very soul, to make sure Farley got what he deserved.

She wanted nothing more than to stop Farley. Keep

him from harming others. But not at anyone else's expense.

Certainly not at Travis's.

"Please, Travis," she pleaded softly, unsure what to say. "I'm all right. You don't need to—"

"But *you*, Ms. Englander, need to learn to listen. You agreed you wouldn't go anywhere without letting me know first."

"But I did. I—"

"Yeah, you called when it was too late for me to get here. Damn it, you could have been killed."

"I wasn't, though. I—"

She didn't finish. She couldn't finish, for he had grasped her tightly by the arms. She had only an instant to pull away as his blue eyes, blazing and brilliant and glazed with passion, captivated hers.

She didn't pull away. Instead, she tilted her chin and waited for his kiss.

She wasn't disappointed.

ALL COMMON SENSE HAD disappeared from Travis. He knew it. Its flight had left him with no more control than a rutting animal.

He could no more have kept himself from kissing Dianna than he could have made himself actually disappear into a puff of smoke—though he'd performed that illusion many times.

He had no illusions now. No tricks up his sleeve.

He simply wanted Dianna. Living, breathing.

Safe.

He lowered his head and covered her mouth with his.

He heard a tiny noise that might signify he was hurting her, but when he tried to pull back he found himself encircled by her arms, his face held right there where he wanted it.

Kissing Dianna.

Her lips were every bit as soft as he'd imagined, but there was nothing wimpy about the way she tasted him, even as he let his tongue work its magic exploring her lips, the inside of her mouth, the dancing, darting teasing of her tongue in return.

He let his hands range over her back. Holding her near. Feeling her sway against him, where she couldn't help but feel how rock-hard she was making him. He gripped her buttocks, pulling her closer still.

Heard her moan again even as he felt the vibration of the sound against his mouth.

Heard the sound of a car's tires shrilling against concrete...

He pulled back. "We're in a damned parking lot," he growled, even as he looked down into the languid bewilderment in Dianna's soft blue eyes.

Her expression adjusted immediately to awareness. A hint of embarrassment.

He hadn't meant the kiss. Neither had she.

Well, not exactly true. He *had* meant it. If they hadn't been in the damned garage, he might even have done something about it, no matter how stupid it was.

After all, he'd already admitted to himself that the situation had sent his common sense out the door, leaving only his animal instincts.

The car he'd heard pulled into a space a few down from where they stood.

"Okay, Dianna, enough of maintaining my cover. Let's get a crime team here." He spoke in a soft, composed voice as she continued to regard him warily, then angrily. But better that she think it an act than real. *Really* kissing her was a real bad idea.

But after that kiss, her full lips looked nearly as bruised as her neck. That didn't make him feel guilty. Only more needy.

"No crime team." Her protest sounded irate, not hurt. Good. "I need to get to Julie's school."

"Soon," he promised. He made a cell phone call. As he waited to get through, he asked Dianna, "Sure you're okay? Should I have them send EMTs?"

She shook her head. "I'm fine." Her voice was still hoarse, belying what she said, but she was one hell of a brave lady. And a kisser *par excellence*.

Great for his cover. *Remember that, Bronson.*

She held up well, too, when a detective arrived, along with some SID crime-scene guys. The techs took hair samples, her prints, her photo. They got her key off the floor and took blood samples from her fingers, too. The detective asked a lot of questions. She didn't collapse. Nor did she hold her temper.

"It was Glen Farley!" she erupted in response to the interrogation. "Check his blood and fingerprints and whatever else you find against all the evidence on record in the other cases where he was implicated."

"It's just a formality," Travis soothed. But he understood.

He knew her history. Read the few files the feds had deigned to allow the lowly LAPD in on under current policies of sharing—sometimes.

Her credibility had been assumed at first, after she'd ID'd Farley in the murder of her husband. They'd had Farley's picture, since he'd sent threatening letters to her husband, and she'd picked him out from a group. They'd bought the ID, since there was corroborating physical evidence. But they'd found no backup to her later claims that the SOB Farley was harassing her. She'd been labeled hysterical each time she'd declared she'd spotted Farley. Ten times or so, she'd reported his accosting her. Ten times, the files indicated, she'd been handled with kid gloves like the VIP widow she was…but her claims were ignored.

Hysteria? Travis didn't think so, not since he'd met her.

Besides, someone had blown up the redevelopment site near the Convention Center in downtown L.A.

Someone had left the ticking present on her desk.

Worst of all, someone had attacked her here. Today.

He could have prevented it, if he'd been with her.

Next time, he *would* be with her. As a smitten push-cart driver and eager, oversexed juggler who wanted her patronage.

The techs were done. They kept her key, but she fortunately retrieved a spare from inside her purse.

Travis approached her, where she leaned against her cool little red car, and held out his hand. She looked down at it, then quizzically back at his face.

"Your key," he said, answering her unspoken question. "You're going to Julie's school, and I'm driving. It's part of the service."

She looked at first as if she were going to protest. But her hesitation lasted only a moment. He figured it was all in the glare. *No protests this time, lady. Wherever you go, I go.*

She handed him the key. Nice car. He'd enjoy driving it.

Almost as much as, what now felt like eons before, he'd enjoyed kissing its owner.

DIANNA KEPT her mind occupied, as Travis drove her car, by giving him directions. At least more or less occupied.

He'd kissed her.

No, she'd kissed him. Out of relief that she was still alive. And because…well, because she'd wanted to. That once. Now that her curiosity had been assuaged, she wouldn't have to do that again. His *cover* notwithstanding.

Right. Give her an opportunity, and—

"So you told me before that you were dashing off to Julie's school," Travis said, interrupting her thoughts, "and that she was in some kind of trouble, but what you didn't explain was why *you.* Where's her dad?"

"Beth couldn't find her." It was becoming easier to talk after her ordeal, though still painful, and her voice sounded deep and scratchy.

"I heard her mother's no longer in the picture," Travis said. "Something about an accident?"

Dianna nodded and swallowed to moisten her throat. "It happened before I was hired by A-S, but I heard about it. So tragic… Millie—she was Wally's sister as well as Jeremy's wife—apparently had a little too much to drink at a party and fell down the stairs when she got home. Her neck was broken." She shuddered. "Fortunately, Jeremy found her, not Julie. If she'd seen her mom that way—"

"Yeah." Something in Travis's voice made Dianna glance at him, but his expression was blank as he watched the road.

To fill the uncomfortable silence, Dianna continued, "I heard she worked nearly next door to Englander Center, in the Department of Building and Safety, did something with building permits. Of course the center wasn't completed then, but it would have been so convenient for both Jeremy and Millie—commuting together. Grabbing lunch now and then…''

The car made a sharp turn, and despite her seat belt, Dianna had to brace herself, which made her sore body ache. Travis had pulled onto the school's twisting drive. Dianna's thoughts moved to the meeting—no, confrontation— to come.

Beverly Pacifica Middle School was a private institution hugging the south side of the Santa Monica Mountains near Mulholland Drive. The campus had a view of Bel Air and Beverly Hills. Dianna had no doubt that Julie's tuition set Jeremy Alberts back as much as if she attended a private university.

Travis pulled into the parents' parking lot and looked at the vast pink hacienda-style building that housed the school's administration as well as some classrooms. His low whistle caressed her spine. She'd already been attracted to the rich depth of his voice. Was his whistle, too, going to tease her with what else he might do well with those sexy lips?

''Nice place,'' said that sensuous voice. ''Don't suppose it's one of the L.A. Unified School District's well-kept secrets?''

''No, it's the well-endowed competition.'' Dianna tossed him a grin before opening the door.

He got out of the car. Rather, he unfurled. Travis was an inch or two over six feet, and he'd had to scrunch a bit to fit behind her steering wheel, even with the seat pushed all the way back. He hadn't seemed to mind. In fact, she'd almost caught him purring as he'd driven her high-powered little auto. At least the grin on his face on most of the route had suggested he was an instant away from humming his rapture aloud.

Men and wheels! But she couldn't blame him. She loved her car, too.

And this time, she had to unfurl as well, for a different reason. She ached all over, and not just around her throat, where Farley had squeezed…. She shuddered and turned up her blouse's collar. No need to advertise her bruises here.

Travis was beside her in an instant, one strong arm around her shoulders. "You sure you're okay?"

"Yes," she asserted. Maybe it was a lie, but she wasn't about to tell him she still felt like melting like a ball of putty and sinking into her bed at home. He'd issue her orders to do just that. "You don't need to come in with me. I'm only going to see the principal."

"What? And make me miss this opportunity to see where the rich kids go to school? Not on your life."

He spoke lightly, but she sensed something more behind it. She hadn't gotten Travis to tell her much about himself, where he came from, but doubted he'd been one of those "rich kids" whose environment he now wanted to see.

They had to pass through a security check, and then they were shown into an elegant, antique-filled waiting room. No mundane magazines like *People* or *Good Housekeeping* here. Instead, back issues of *Architectural Digest* and *Paris Match* were carefully arranged on the Victorian teak coffee table.

Julie was waiting for them. She sat on a stiff but equally ornate chair, head down, one toe of her designer tennis shoes making divots in the plush cream-colored carpet. She wore pink jeans and a matching frilly top, and looked even younger than her eleven years. Some of her long brown hair had, as usual, escaped its barrette, so it wisped around her face.

She looked up sullenly as Dianna and Travis entered the room, then brightened as she recognized them, leaping out of her seat. "Dianna. You came! And you brought the magician." She looked a little puzzled at that, which didn't surprise Dianna.

"This is Travis," she told the girl. "He was nice enough to come along because—"

As she fumbled for a good reason, Travis stepped in. "Because I'm working on the entertainment for the Englander Center's birthday celebration."

"Oh, good!" Julie clapped her hands in excitement—just as the inner door to the office opened. Immediately, her body stiffened and her gaze flew to the floor once more.

The woman who emerged was petite but her presence filled the room. "Good afternoon. I am Mrs. Kinch." Evidently no first names were to be used here. "Are you Ms. Englander?" Her hair formed a neat cap on her head. Its silvery iron color suggested she was middle-aged or older, but there were no lines on her formidably expressionless face.

"Yes, I am."

Mrs. Kinch turned toward Travis, obviously expecting an introduction. The stark formality of her black suit contrasted almost humorously with his informal jeans and work shirt. Dianna opened her mouth to introduce Travis, but he strode forward, hand outstretched. "Delighted to meet you, Mrs. Kinch. Julie has spoken so fondly of you."

Her eyes widened as if in amazement, but she quickly caught herself. "Thank you…er, Mr.—"

"Bronson. I'm a good friend of Julie's family's. Like Dianna…er, Ms. Englander."

"Well, then, please come in."

Dianna, having been married to a U.S. Representative, was a veteran of some highly uncomfortable political situations, but that hadn't prepared her for the next, painful ten minutes.

They sipped coffee from tiny cups that had to be Limoges. The heat soothed Dianna's throat but did no good at all in soothing her growing temper. Travis and she were subjected to the most vituperative of diatribes against Julie, right in the child's presence and spoken in a cool monotone. Mrs. Kinch had set the rules ahead of time. She was to speak, they were to listen, and then they would have their say.

Julie was definitely on her most disfavored student list. "We have a special parent-student day coming up next month," Mrs. Kinch intoned, "the Mother Festival, and she has already been most disruptive about it. I realize her situation is…different, but that is no excuse. She starts fights with the other students, and—" She shot a glare at Julie, who had shifted in her seat, obviously ready to defend herself. The child's breathing quickened, but she returned her gaze to the glass of juice in her hand.

The woman expounded on the arguments and physical altercations Julie had allegedly caused. When she was through, she looked at Dianna expectantly with an imperious gaze, as if anticipating her abject apology and promise that she would ensure that nothing like this would happen again.

Instead, Dianna went and knelt beside the child. When Julie glanced sidelong at her, Dianna saw moisture in her eyes.

She was about to ask Julie for her side when Travis, who crouched on Julie's other side, said, "Sounds like this little girl needs some discipline, doesn't it?"

Shocked and furious, Dianna rose, only to see a glint in his eyes as he regarded the principal that made her both worry and stifle a grin at the same time.

"Now, the way I look at it," he continued, "this is a school for kids who have opinions—*yours.*"

Indignation paled Mrs. Kinch's face. "I—"

"No, ma'am, you've had your turn. Now it's time for Julie's side. Honey, you tell us what's been happening around here."

"The kids are mean!" Julie shouted, then looked guiltily at the principal, whose glare was cold enough to turn the coffees into cappuccino slush.

"How are they mean?" Dianna asked softly.

Tears of anger flowed down her cheeks as Julie described the special parent-children day that was planned. "Mostly kids are bringing their mothers in the morning, their stepmothers in the afternoon. Lots of them are divorced, you know?"

Dianna nodded solemnly. She did know how many children came from broken homes. That was one reason Englander Center existed—to help in the legal end of divorce. The emotional end...well, that was a lot harder.

"But I don't have a mother or stepmother," Julie wailed, "and some kids make fun of me and the others who don't have either. I tell them what creeps they are, and sometimes they hit me, so I hit back."

"I see." Travis's tone was much too calm. "So the way I see it, Mrs. Kinch, you've got a problem here: mean kid syndrome. I suggest you fix it quick, or I'm going to recommend that Julie's dad withdraw her and all that nice tuition money he's paying. And not quietly, either. Maybe some other parents will want to hear how you don't deal with mean kid syndrome." He cocked his head as he stared at the obviously fuming principal.

"Not to worry, ma'am. You just need to hire a counselor or two. And here's a good way to start paying for it."

She flinched as he reached toward her.

It wasn't just a quarter he made a show of extracting from the side jacket of her suit coat, but a hundred dollar bill.

Julie squealed in delight, and even Dianna had to laugh.

Travis grinned irrepressibly. "And now, Julie, come with us. It's almost time for your juggling lesson."

"YOU ARE TOO COOL, Travis," Julie said as they headed for the school cafeteria. She'd asked for some more fruit juice before they went home, and Dianna had agreed.

Travis had a feeling that the kid just wanted to show the bratty pipsqueaks around here that she had friends, too.

She pranced between Dianna and him, holding their hands. Travis liked the feeling. He liked being called "too cool."

Not that he'd ever wanted to be around kids much. He'd been around enough to last a lifetime when *he* was a kid in the system. There'd been no one to take his side when he was in one foster home after another. He hated to see a kid hurting, the way he had.

"I hope your daddy's not too mad at me if I've gotten you kicked out of school," he told Julie. It wouldn't be much of a loss. Not that he was a good judge, but he hated to see what a snobby education would do a sweet kid like Julie.

"I guess not," Julie said quietly. "I don't want to be here for the Mother Festival anyway. Unless—" She looked over at Dianna. "Could you come and be like my mother, Dianna?"

"Well…" They'd reached the cafeteria door.

"I know my daddy likes you," Julie continued, tugging the door open. "Maybe someday you really could be my mother." She walked in, leaving Dianna staring after her, looking like she'd been sucker-punched.

Travis, too, felt like punching someone. Jeremy Alberts, maybe, though the guy wasn't here to defend himself. But Travis had seen the way he looked at Dianna.

A short while later, they each had peach nectar in front of them as they sat at long, gouged wooden tables that didn't look like they belonged within a hundred miles of that witchy principal's elegant domicile. Only a few tables were occupied, all adults, probably staff on break, though Travis figured the place would fill with screaming midgets at noon, an hour away.

"Honey," Dianna began, "what you said before about—"

"About you being my mother? You'd have to marry my dad. I'll bet that would be okay with him." Her tone was casual, but the twerp looked as if she was holding her breath.

So was Travis. Jeremy Alberts was an okay guy, if stodgy, but he certainly wasn't good enough for Dianna. No one was, in Travis's book. *He* most certainly wasn't.…

"Julie, when people get married, it's because they feel something very special for one another. Your daddy's a nice man, but—"

"But you don't have the hots for him. I figured that." She brushed a hank of hair from her face and took a sip of juice.

Travis had to bite on his lip to keep from laughing out loud. How was Dianna going to handle that one?

"At your age, what do you know about that?" she blurted.

"I watch TV and the movies," Julie said maturely.

"More than you should," Dianna agreed. "But you—"

"What's that on your neck?" Julie interrupted, reaching toward Dianna and pulled down her collar. "Did you hurt yourself?" Her voice rose. "Are you okay, Dianna? Did you fall down the stairs?" The kid sounded hysterical.

Dianna scooted closer to Julie and took her into her arms. "I did get hurt a little this morning, honey, but I'm fine. It was…an accident, but I didn't fall down the stairs like your mom did."

Travis couldn't help feeling bad for the kid. He knew what it was like to lose a parent. Both, in fact. A brother, too.

"Tell you what," Dianna said. "I'll tell Mrs. Kinch that she needs to change the name of the Mother Festival. It'll be the 'Mother and Aunt Festival,' and I'm going to come as your aunt Dianna. How will that be?"

Travis wasn't into mush, but his insides gooed up like nothing he'd ever felt before as Julie dove into Dianna's arms and hugged her. He couldn't help it. He drew closer and put his arms around them both.

Damn, but that felt good.

For now, for this moment, he allowed himself to wonder what belonging, having a family, might be like.

GLEN FARLEY FLASHED a driver's license at the asses manning the security system at Englander Center. It read Randolph Jones, showed an address in Santa Clarita, California—north of the San Fernando Valley—and had a picture that resembled him. For the moment. He'd shaved his head to look bald and wore a prosthetic gadget in his mouth to give him buck teeth. Not to mention the tiny, dark glasses perched on his nose.

Plus, he'd hidden the deep, fresh scratch along his face with a generous helping of well-applied makeup.

He smiled at the head guy, Cal Flynn, who gave a not-so-friendly nod. Not even Flynn recognized him.

Farley slipped into the elevator with all the other saps who'd been allowed into the building and rode to the top floor. He got out and, making sure he looked as if he knew exactly where he was going, headed for one of the pretend courtrooms at the end of the hall.

Not that he needed to right now. But he loved the challenge of slipping in and out whenever he felt like it. As he had in the parking garage this morning. He'd had Dianna Englander right in his hands. He felt a hard-on at the recollection of how she had felt. How she had gasped for air…

But he nearly growled aloud thinking about what she had done to him. He touched his cheek, then quickly lowered his hand.

Going back downstairs, he headed for the bank in the lobby. The nearest branch had been dislocated when Englander Center was built. Damn rich institution had no problem closing down for a while, then coming right on back, money-grubbing as ever.

Not so all the little businesses displaced by someone's big, fat redevelopment idea. Like his was once.

He reached the head of the line. "Hi," he said to the teller, a young kid, probably still in college. "I'd like to cash this check." And to case this joint. Isn't that how the old crooks used to say it?

"Of course, sir."

Good thing he'd been in the security business. He'd

learned all the tricks while fighting them from the legitimate side of the system. He passed his false ATM card through the scanner, pressed in a PIN number, and was handed a hundred bucks in crisp twenties—money from someone else's account that would help, with what else he was getting, to finance the end of this branch.

The end of Englander Center.

How he loved what he did now! Maybe he should have thanked Brad Englander for ruining his life. Otherwise, how would he have known how much he enjoyed fooling people, blowing things up?

Killing people.

Most of all, right now, he loved terrorizing Dianna. He'd get rid of her soon. Probably should have done it before, since she was the only person who knew what he really looked like.

And she hated him. Really hated him. She'd love to kill *him*.

Not that he'd give her the opportunity. But he wanted her to suffer a little more.

After all, that was part of his game. It was fun.

And it was particularly enjoyable, since, this time, his game was going to make him very, very rich.

''Thanks, and have a nice day,'' he said to the smiling teller, and left the bank.

Chapter Eight

"That's it, ladies," Travis said. "You're doing fine."

Yeah, definitely, he thought. Especially Dianna.

They were in an empty office in the A-S Development suite—Dianna, Julie and him. After they brought Julie here from school, Dianna had shown them into it, then insisted on helping him move the unoccupied desk and chairs closer to a wall so they'd have space without worrying about hitting anything.

He'd brought basic equipment from where he kept it now, on a shelf at the base of Manny's cart. Among other stuff, the cardboard box contained a few balls and several clubs. Once they were settled in, he'd shown them the simplest of juggling moves—one ball, throwing it up in the air and catching it with the other hand, over and over. Only when that was mastered could a potential juggler graduate to adding another ball. Then another.

To Travis's surprise, not only Julie had decided to give it a try. Dianna, too, had wanted a juggling lesson.

And she was doing damn well at it. She'd mastered one ball nearly immediately, graduating to two. She winced now and then, but if she hurt from the attack on her earlier, she didn't let it stop her. She tossed the balls now, one at a time, from her right hand to her left, from her left hand into the air, keeping them moving. Keeping her body moving, her fluid motions lifting her short blue skirt higher. Showing even more of her slender, sexy thighs...

He'd thought this office was large enough for all of them to practice. Now, it felt no bigger than a closet. Dianna was too close to him.

Not close enough.

Good thing she was concentrating on her actions. Otherwise, she might notice that he, too, was concentrating on *her*.

He made himself look again at Julie. "Keep going. You're doing great." With just one ball, but that was fine. She was only a kid.

As she practiced, Julie's small brow was crinkly in concentration, her mouth slightly open. Cute. But definitely not on the same level of noteworthiness as Dianna.

At least, it looked as if Julie had put the words of that crumb of a principal behind her, at least for now. Travis wished he could forget the stuff he'd hated that day as easily. That SOB Farley had attacked Dianna. She was okay, which was the good part. But Travis hadn't been with her. She'd gone through that terror alone. Because she hadn't listened to him.

"How am I doing?" Dianna broke into his thoughts.

"Great." His irritation with her, with what had happened, turned the word into a sarcastic growl, but quickly he repeated, "Just great," meaning it. She was one hell of a natural, working with two balls as gracefully and effortlessly as if she'd juggled most of her life—as he'd done. "Want to try three balls?"

"What about knives?" She glanced toward him with a wobbly smile—and that small breach of concentration was enough. Both balls tumbled from the air. She caught one.

"Don't think you want to do that with knives," he said.

Julie giggled.

"You're right." Dianna's lush mouth curled in obvious dismay. "But..." She didn't finish the thought, but he figured he knew what she'd been thinking. The lesson had probably been meant as a distraction, to keep her thoughts off what had happened earlier—both Julie's ordeal and her own. It hadn't completely worked. Maybe she'd assumed, if she learned to juggle knives, she'd feel more in control of her own protection.

But it took time to work up to something as jazzy, as risky, as twirling blades.

"Tell you what. We'll try the next best thing." He reached into his box. "Start with clubs. When you get good enough with them, you can substitute catching their necks with knife hilts."

"Oh, yeah!" Dianna grinned in such pleased anticipation that he wanted to grab her, twirl her in his arms.

Maybe even give her a big kiss...

"Will you teach us card tricks, too?" Julie asked. She'd stopped tossing her ball and looked at him hopefully.

"Sure." Glad for the diversion, he pulled a deck from his box. He fanned them out and told Julie to pick one. Using one of his easiest techniques, he told her to put it back, then identified it for her. The child exclaimed in delight.

"Did you use a marked deck?" Dianna asked. Her accusatory expression told him she was thinking of the deck he had used with her previously—the one with "Beware" on every card.

He grinned. "Not this time." He showed Julie how he'd shuffled the cards carefully, making certain their order didn't get changed at all. That way, he could figure out right away which card had been hers. It was one of the simplest of tricks, but it delighted the child.

"Let me practice," Julie said.

"Sure." Travis handed her the deck.

"My turn again," Dianna said with a wry grin so sexy it made Travis's pulse pound. "Teach me how to juggle clubs."

"Right." Travis showed her how to hold a club, not too far down the handle. This close, her soft scent, as spicy as exotic flowers, was nearly intoxicating. He touched her hands while showing her the grip. They were warm. Smooth. And as she clutched the club's handle, her fingers gave him all sorts of ideas of how they'd feel on his...

"Now what?" she asked. Her eyes met his, and he could see the pinkness tingeing her face, as if she read his thoughts.

Slowly, very slowly, he removed his hands from hers. "Like this." He showed her how to toss the club into the air, catching it with the other hand.

She practiced for a minute, but her timing was off. Maybe that was because she kept sneaking glances at him that made him feel as hot as if the clubs were lighted torches.

"Show us how you juggle three clubs," Julie commanded him, still holding the deck of cards.

"Sure." And while he did, he watched what he was doing instead of Dianna.

"How soon can I do that?" Dianna demanded, disrupting his concentration.

"Soon enough. I'll teach you, but you'll have to practice."

"Of course."

He believed her. And he *wanted* to teach her… juggling. That was all.

Damn. His timing was off. He nearly missed a catch. He grabbed all the clubs from the air. Enough was enough. He needed to leave before he ruined his timing totally. He might never get it back, if every toss, every catch, reminded him of Dianna.

"Gotta go," he told them. "But I'll see you later. Hang onto the clubs if you'd like. The cards, too. Keep practicing."

"Thanks, Travis," Julie said.

"Yes, thanks." Dianna's words followed him into the suite's short hallway. But he couldn't really leave, damn it. Not altogether.

Dianna was there. She'd been attacked that day. He hadn't been there to help, and he had to atone for it. For nearly failing her. Too reminiscent of old times. Of Cassi, and how he had cared for her, and how his distraction from duty had killed her.

Quickly he made a call on his cell phone.

"THIS IS Officer Philip Kelbart Ashburn the Third," Travis said.

Dianna stood still behind her desk to minimize her soreness from the attack, for it had been exacerbated by the juggling lesson. A nice-looking, slightly-built young guy had just joined them in her office.

"Call me Snail, Ms. Englander," he said, solemnity and deference written all over his sincere face. His complexion was tanned golden-brown.

"You can call me Dianna," she responded with a

smile he tentatively mirrored, "if you tell me why you're called Snail."

"Because he's the fastest runner in my group of officers," Travis responded. "And the guys in 'L' Platoon are picked not just for their good looks, but for their skills. Some can play street performers, like me, do tricks while working a crowd. Others can hide in a crowd, then run quicker than the bad guys expect. Snail's even caught a suspect by running up to his driver's door and extracting him from his moving vehicle."

"Impressive." Dianna caught Travis's pointed gaze and knew what he was thinking. Too bad Snail hadn't been with her that morning in the parking garage.

Maybe Farley wouldn't have gotten away.

But there were a lot of maybes she could think of, and the most significant of all was: *Maybe* she shouldn't have been there alone in the first place.

"Snail's my backup," Travis said. "I've got to go work on my cover down on the plaza. Snail, here, is a good temporary secretary, believe it or not. I've already cleared with Jeremy that you need one. So—"

Dianna closed her eyes and began counting. "So you've decided how to make sure someone is here to be my nursemaid."

"Oh, but isn't he a cute nursemaid?"

Dianna watched a slow flush rise up Snail's face. It was angular, hinted of a beard beneath his tanned cheeks, but its thinness and lack of crinkles suggested he was a neophyte at the cop game.

"Yes, he's a very nice-looking man. In fact, maybe it'll be a pleasure having him here." She saw Travis's eyes narrow. Why? That kiss hadn't given him any possessory rights over her.

"Right." Travis's voice was gruff. "You keep close tabs on her, Snail. The rest room is off limits, but you stand outside if she heads there. Otherwise—"

"I'm not going to put up with that kind of baby-sitting!" Dianna didn't mean to shout her frustration that way, but it came out anyway.

"Yeah, you are," Travis said levelly, his blue eyes flashing their command along with his lips.

Those sexy lips that had kissed her before…

She was brought starkly back to reality, though, as he finished his thought. "Your friend Farley isn't about to listen if I tell him not to stalk you anymore. So, Ms. Englander, if you want to stay alive and healthy, you need to learn to follow my orders."

Before she could think of a suitable retort, Travis strode from her office. Only then did she realize how quivery her knees had become. She sank into her chair.

She met Snail's uncomfortable yet sympathetic gaze. The poor young cop actually reported to officious, over-bearing Travis Bronson. Maybe he, too, had been the subject of Travis's infernal domineering.

"So, Snail," Dianna said as conversationally as she was able, "how long have you worked for that big bully?"

Snail grinned and shrugged one shoulder. "Not long enough, ma'am. I think bossiness comes with my next set of lessons."

THIS LATE in the afternoon, on the plaza outside Englander Center, people were just beginning to dribble from the civic center buildings.

Most ignored Travis, though he stood there, right beside Manny Fernandez's brightly-painted snack cart, juggling six-inch steak knives.

He had become part of the scenery. Fine with him. His job was to watch the passersby. Their job, as far as he was concerned, was to go about their business.

Except for Farley. *His* job was to mess up. Get caught. *Now.*

"Hey, mister, you ever cut yourself?" An adolescent boy, whose attempt to look uninterested had failed miserably, stopped in front of him.

Cut himself? Never! But thinking about Dianna that way had distracted him so that the kid's voice had actually startled him.

"Did you ever cut yourself?" the boy insisted.

Travis did his customary assessment: Kid from the local high school, probably, on his way home. With a group of friends who'd stopped, too, so he had to look cool.

"Nope, never even a scratch. I'm good."

The kid's dark eyes narrowed in a grin of appreciation as he walked on with his buddies.

"You got an ego, too," said Manny, who'd just handed an older lady a cappuccino. Manny was leather-skinned and middle-aged, and his family owned one of the small coffee shops along Van Nuys Boulevard. He'd told Travis he'd jumped at the chance to run the cart, since it kept him out in the nice, smoggy Los Angeles air instead of inside with his squabbling brothers.

"Who says?" Travis turned so his knives could slice a nice chunk out of the man who'd helped him establish his cover here. Could, but wouldn't. Travis had them under complete control as he tossed four, catching each in turn by its handles and casting it back into the air so the blade flashed but never neared his flesh or anyone else's.

Manny smiled his pumpkin grin. "Tomorrow I'll

bring tomatoes from the restaurant that you can slice for me, okay?'' He nodded at the glinting knives.

"Sure. I'm easy."

"Now, though," Manny said, "I'm ready to go home."

A while later, after helping Manny pack up the cart and wheel it away, Travis returned to his corner of the walkway outside Englander Center.

Twilight approached, and with it came the chill of evening. He was active enough not to feel cold, despite the way he'd rolled up the sleeves of his shirt. He had to make allowances in his tosses, though, for a slight, but burgeoning, breeze.

His knives flipped and landed easily in his palms with a faint slapping sound, only to be tossed again to make room for the next. He probably looked out of his element, without Manny and the cart to lend him legitimacy—an entertainer drawing attention to a vendor. He caught the gazes of passersby more frequently now, when they couldn't ignore him as part of the place's commercial ambiance. A few tossed coins, which he would donate to charity when this was over. Eyes in every shade studied him. Acknowledged him. Some even appreciated him.

None, he was certain, were Farley's. No slyness. No furtiveness. No pretense.

Travis was relaxed, yes. But he maintained his vigilance.

And then he saw Dianna.

Though wilted-looking after her tough day, she smiled at him. Her blue skirt and light blouse had held up better than the rest of her, for her shoulders slumped, and beneath her eyes was a bruiselike darkness of exhaustion.

Tired, drooping from fatigue, whatever, she was still one pretty lady.

Travis's muscles tensed, though not enough to make him lose his rhythm. His blood already flowed heatedly as a result of concentration and motion. The smile that brightened Dianna's weary face made him even more conscious of its circulation.

Its flow to body parts that had nothing to do with juggling.

She drew closer. She wasn't alone, of course. Snail was with her. The kid was diligent. He stood behind Dianna, then edged around nonchalantly, as if he'd nothing better to do. But he was alert. Travis knew that artless pose. He assumed it himself, often. For Snail *did* have something better to do—shielding Dianna from an unseen foe.

This time, when the hilts of Travis's knives reached his palms, he held them. His juggling for this day was done.

"Good evening, Ms. Englander," he said. "I'm calling it a day. You, too?" He still played the role of a routine juggler, deferential to the executive with control over his fate. Ms. Englander could invite him to continue his act, or tell him to move on.

As if he would allow the latter.

"Yes," she responded. "Jeremy's still upstairs with Julie. He's got one more appointment today—a possible subcontractor. But I'm going home. It's been a long one."

That's right, Travis thought with a scowl, gazing around. *Announce to the world where you're heading.*

Of course, Farley would know she'd head home. Travis made himself relax again.

"Have a good evening," he said, then watched her saunter toward the parking lot.

Snail stayed with her. "So tonight I'll help you organize those files you wanted at your house, Ms. Englander." Right. The kid's cover was, after all, as a temporary secretary.

Juggling beat that any day.

But there had to be a reason for the undercover cop to accompany their subject home. Organizing her personal files seemed flimsy, but what the heck?

Except that the idea of someone else spending the night in Dianna's home didn't sit well with Travis. Not even Snail.

A short while later, he shadowed them in his Jeep, though not too closely. Far as he could tell, he was the only one following.

And Travis knew well how to spot a tail.

Soon, as they'd arranged in advance, he pulled into the parking lot of a mini-mall a few blocks away. Dianna's little red sports car had already slid into a parking space in front of a dry cleaners, and beside it was Snail's car, a clunky, five-year-old sedan. Travis, his eyes still surveilling the road, approached Dianna's car. So did Snail.

"Is everything under control?" she asked after opening her window.

"Looks that way."

"Good." She glanced over her shoulder toward Snail. "So it's okay for me to take my baby-sitter home now?"

"No, the plans have changed," Travis said, surprising them all, including himself. "After that episode earlier, I think you need to discuss the entertainment for the Englander Center birthday bash with the area's best juggler."

"But you said—" Snail began. At a look from Travis, he shut up.

"Don't you have a date tonight?" Travis growled.

"Not yet, but I will," Snail said enthusiastically. Travis caught Dianna's half amused, half irritated grimace. "I don't really need to discuss files, juggling or anything else tonight." Her tone rang with barely repressed exasperation. "Can't you just have someone watch my place again tonight—outside?"

"We'll do that, too," Travis said, "but Farley's getting bolder. He didn't just play peek-a-boo with you today. And I've no doubt he knows where you live. So, no, Dianna. You're going to have someone hang around inside—at least for tonight. *Me.*"

DIANNA WOULDN'T ADMIT IT, but after the way Farley had grabbed her earlier, she was glad Travis would be with her. She trusted him. At least she trusted him to keep her safe. *If* she followed his damned overbearing orders. But what choice did she have?

She still felt unnerved after that morning's attack. Her body had been weak with soreness and anxiety the entire day. Not that she'd given in to it.

They'd grabbed a quick sandwich from a fast food place in the shopping center. Now, as she settled back into her driver's seat, she recognized that having Travis with her that night, for protection, would be a relief.

And a temptation to make part of his cover all too real—the part that said the street performer was hitting on the building executive. Or vice versa.

She glanced into her rearview mirror. The silver Jeep he drove had pulled from the parking lot and now followed her, a few cars behind. Obviously trying to be protective, but unobtrusive.

As if the sexy, handsome juggler could ever be unobtrusive.

All this stuff with Farley must be driving her crazy, for she'd never felt so sexually aware of a man in her life as with Travis.

She pushed the button on her steering wheel, and the car was suddenly filled with a recent tune played by her favorite soft rock radio station. She drummed a finger on the leather cover in time with the music. The rhythm reminded her of sex, which reminded her of Travis...

Oh, she'd loved Brad. Their lovemaking had been enjoyable, for he'd waged a campaign with his body the same way as he had a political campaign—personably. Intellectually. As if he had to impress the world with his abilities.

Dianna sensed Travis wouldn't give a damn about impressing anyone. He wouldn't plan; he'd *do*. Spontaneously. He'd use his sleight-of-hand skills to tease and taunt and—

Damn. She'd almost missed the turnoff to her narrow street, up in the hills. Sheepishly, she slowed and directed her car to climb along homes shrouded by tall palms, twisting eucalyptus and wild bougainvillea overgrowing solid picket fences.

She pulled down her driveway, using the electronic button to open her garage door. Her little car rumbled as she eased it into its space. She glanced again into her rearview mirror. Travis didn't try to pull in behind her.

Where was he now?

She reminded herself that she didn't like the idea that he'd followed her home to protect her. She just wanted to be left alone. She just wanted—

She jumped as a shadow appeared behind her. But she calmed as she recognized that tall, substantial form. The way Travis always stood, relaxed, yet poised as if to leap on an enemy and slit his throat with one of his lethal-looking juggling knives.

He opened the car door for her. "You ready for another juggling lesson?" he asked. "I've also been thinking about some other guys we can get to perform on the plaza for the Center's birthday. None juggles as well as me, but they're all great undercover cops."

"Right." She tried to sound disgruntled, but she actually wasn't. She didn't like this undercover stuff, figured Farley would see through it, but what if he did? The idea was to keep her safe—and to catch the miserable wretch. He was most likely insane, but that didn't mean he was stupid. To the contrary, he seemed much too smart. He'd probably figured she was under police protection. If so, he apparently considered it a challenge, for he had come after her anyway.

Might come after her again…

Shrugging away that chilling thought, she hurried to unlock the door from the garage into her kitchen, flicked on the light and hurried inside to press in her alarm code within the grace period before it went off.

And gasped, even as she heard Travis swear aloud.

Her kitchen had been trashed. Plates, glasses, flatware, small appliances—everything was in a shattered heap on the hardwood floor.

And spray-painted in bright red paint on the walnut cabinets were the words, *You're going to die, bitch.*

Chapter Nine

"Oh, no," Dianna moaned. On top of the nearest pile were the shards of an antique, handpainted canister set. The heirloom wedding present from Brad's family was now nothing but broken remnants, just as her marriage had been crushed by that horrible creature Farley. She took a step into the destroyed room and reached for one of the pieces.

Travis grabbed her, stopping her. "Don't touch anything."

"But—"

"I need to get the SID techs here. They'll know of someone to help clean this mess once they've collected evidence."

Dianna made herself stand stiffly, when all she wanted to do was fall to her knees on the shreds that had been part of her life. "Why do they need evidence?" she whispered brokenly. "We know who did this." She swallowed, becoming aware for the first time of the nauseating odor permeating the room—a conglomeration of all the things pulled from the open refrigerator-freezer and hurled into a congealing mess on the floor. She couldn't help the small keening noise that emanated from her throat—which was just healing from Farley's *last* onslaught. "What does he want from me?" she wailed.

She would have slid to the floor if Travis hadn't wrapped his strong arms around her. "He wants to scare you," he responded in a tone so low and furious and feral that Dianna drew in her breath, as if he had slapped her. "Let's find you someplace to sit," he said more gently.

He led her carefully around the mess, though she still felt things she could not identify beneath the thin soles of her dressy pumps, heard them slide along the floor and crush. In a moment, they were in the hall, and he ushered her into the den.

"Here." He eased her onto the chair behind her antique walnut desk, also an heirloom from Brad's family. At least everything seemed all right in here.

He called someone on his cell phone, resting one lean hip against the desk. He didn't take his eyes from her, as if he expected her to shatter like the things in the other room that had once been her possessions.

She wouldn't, damn it. Somehow, she would find a way to stop Farley's campaign of terror against her.

She took a deep breath, and then another, willing her heart to stop pounding so hard in her chest. She let herself gaze again into Travis's narrowed blue eyes, as if she could absorb some of his strength from his stare.

Only then did she glance down at her desk. A light blinked on her phone's answering machine, and the digital readout indicated she had received five messages.

She froze. When had she turned her machine on? They were probably the usual hang-ups, but she had to be sure. She wasn't expecting any calls at home. During weekdays, her friends knew to call her at work—sparingly. When she'd seen her neighbor and friend Astrid bundling her kids into her car the morning after they'd been sick, she had told her to come knock at the door if she wanted to chat.

It wouldn't be her family, either. Dianna had spoken with her mother that weekend, as usual. After her father's death ten years earlier, her mom had moved to Florida, where she had met a man five years her junior who loved to travel. The two were in Rome by now. And Dianna's only other relative, her brother Dan, though reliable and a dear in his own way, was a stodgy stockbroker in New York. He had helped her manage Brad's estate and now called every Sunday evening like clockwork. This was a weekday. He wouldn't have called—unless in an emergency. And for that, he had her cell phone number.

Shaking her head, she pushed the button, expecting the mechanical female voice she always heard when the caller hung up: "If you'd like to make a call, please hang up and try again…"

But the first message was eerie laughter. Farley's laughter.

Travis reached over and gripped her hand, without shutting off the answering machine. "You don't need to listen to this," he growled. But he was wrong. She *did* need to listen. She didn't let him steer her from the room.

The second and third messages echoed the first, and Farley's hooting, boisterous laughing carved a chunk out of any sense of well-being Dianna might have retained. According to the machine's automatic time stamp, they had been left shortly after Farley attacked Dianna in the garage that morning.

The fourth was from later in the day. In it, a voice disguised electronically said, "In case you are picking up your messages remotely, Dianna, it's time to come home. I'm waiting for you at your place.''

Oh, lord. He might have been in and out of her house all day, making the mess. Maybe *he* had even turned on the answering machine. And there had been no indication he had set off her burglar alarm even once.

By the time the fifth message started to play, Dianna felt as if all the blood had drained from her body. Tears streamed down her face, but she made no move to wipe them. This message said, in an undisguised voice, ''You're too late, Dianna. You're always going to be too late.'' At the sound of the receiver slamming down, a sob choked Dianna.

Before she realized what she was doing, she reached out. Travis responded. In a moment, she was standing, held tightly against him, his strong arms crushing her in a protective embrace that reminded her how sore her body felt. But she didn't move.

''We'll get him, Dianna,'' Travis said. There was not even a hint of doubt in his voice.

She couldn't reply. She only held on, as if Travis was her only connection with reality. With safety. With sanity.

And for that moment, she was certain he was.

Travis stood in the kitchen doorway, watching the techs sift through the shambles for evidence.

He had regulated his breathing, so it was calm and unhurried. But inside, everything was too fast, too irregular, pressing for the fight that he wouldn't have with Farley…tonight. It would come. He would make sure it came.

He just hoped he could maintain enough control to simply arrest the SOB without maiming him first. Almost unconsciously, he shook his right leg gently, feeling the hardness of the snub-nosed gun in his ankle holster.

"I'm done, Lieutenant."

Travis turned at the brusque female voice. It was the investigator he had left with Dianna. "You have her fingerprints for comparison?" he asked.

The short, plump woman's hair was pulled back in a bun so not a strand moved with her nod.

"Fine." Travis maneuvered around to let her into the kitchen, while he headed down the hall. Dianna was by herself.

Not that Farley was likely to break in and harm her with all this activity around, but who knew what that bastard might do? He'd once owned a small business that sold security systems. His knowledge was probably why he'd gotten in here without setting off Dianna's alarm. He obviously could enter at will. Travis would arrange for her locks to be changed but doubted it would do much good.

In any event, he had no intention of leaving her alone. Not when she'd had so many mind games played on her just today. Not after Farley had clearly intended to destroy any sense of safety she might have.

The hallway was short. It had thickly plastered walls of an irregular texture made to look aged, in keeping with the old European flavor of the house. They were painted bright white. Cheerful. Too cheerful for what had happened here that day.

He didn't stop in the doorway but barged right in.

Dianna still sat behind her desk. Her head was bent as if it was too much trouble for her neck to support it.

Damn. He reminded himself that sappy gestures and he didn't mix, but what he wanted more than anything was to pull her into his arms again. Kiss her so hard and fast that she wouldn't even remember what had been done to her...

Yeah. Right. He'd promised himself to keep his distance from the subject of this mission. And he was going to do that.

He had to. He of all people knew the consequences of getting too involved.

Sure, she had felt damned good with her curves pressed against him before. But it had been an act of comfort only. One not to be repeated. No matter how fast and hot his blood pumped at the recollection.

Dianna must have heard him enter the room, for she straightened. Her pallor gave her beautiful face an almost ethereal quality. Angelic. Especially framed with her halo of soft, light hair.

All the more reason for a devil like him to stay far, far away from her.

"What's wrong?" she asked.

He gave a quick laugh. "Dumb question, after your house was trashed on the same day Farley decided to assault you."

"I didn't mean *me*," she said. "What's wrong with *you?*"

He stopped at the edge of her desk, puzzled. "What do you mean?"

"You were limping. Were you hurt?"

He squeezed his hands so tightly into fists that he cut off his blood's circulation. Damn it all, he hadn't been paying attention. "No, I wasn't hurt." Not for the last twenty-odd years, anyway. But he wasn't going there.

"Are you sure?" she persisted. Her gentle blue eyes were narrowed in concern. For him. As if he needed it.

She was the one who needed consoling. "Yeah," he

replied. "Look, Dianna, do you have someone to stay with tonight? It'll take a while for them to finish."

If she wasn't alone, he could go back to his own place, as long as he left a team outside wherever she stayed. It would be better that way. He'd be able to get himself back under control.

That was essential right now. His damned limp made it more than apparent.

"I don't care," she said. "Glen Farley knows where I live, and he wants me scared. Maybe he wants me to run. Just so he can laugh at me like he did on those messages, and…" She must have heard the rise to her own tone that indicated her emotions needed reining in, for she stopped and took a deep breath. He was as impressed as hell that she managed to calm herself. When she spoke again she sounded controlled. "Obviously killing Brad and…and making me miscarry our baby wasn't enough for him. And all those other people he killed and injured since then—well, he still wants more. He intends to kill me, and that's where you come in." She raised her small but determined chin, even as her lower lip jutted defiantly. "You're going to catch him, Travis. And the only way you can do that is for me not to run away."

Instead of shouting at her, he forced himself to sit slowly, calmly, in the nearest chair in the spacious den. An armchair. The thing was too comfortable. He needed to plant his butt on something hard and solid and torturous.

The woman was either very brave or very foolish or both. She was trusting her life to him.

Of course she didn't know his history.

The smile he forced onto his face nearly cracked it with brittleness. "You ought to know, before you go around making statements like that, that the person I was covering on my last mission didn't make it.''

''What do you mean?''

He gave a small shrug of one shoulder, looking past Dianna to the wide window behind her. Its coppery mini-blinds were closed. ''I was undercover, supposedly protecting a lady in a not-so-nice neighborhood who was being harassed by some raunchy, drug-dealing gang-bangers. I liked Cassi. A lot. *Too* much. Things around her got hot, I got distracted and let her ignore what I'd told her for her protection, and she was killed in a drive-by. End of story.''

He heard Dianna draw in her breath. ''Oh, Travis, I'm so sorry.''

''Yeah, her family was, too.''

She rose. Good. Maybe she was getting smart, about to call downtown, get hold of his superior, Captain Hayden Lee, and demand that he explain why he'd assigned a foul-up jerk like Travis to protect her. Tell him she wanted someone else from the elite undercover ''L'' Platoon of LAPD to watch over her. Someone half-competent.

Instead, she stopped beside his chair. Her hand touched his shoulder. ''I've a feeling you're the best there is. And after an experience like that, you won't let it happen again. Right?''

He froze. Every nerve in his pitiful body seemed centered where she was touching. He was aware of her gentle squeeze. It seemed to caress him more places than just his shoulder. It sure had effects on other areas of his body. His mind swam with the idea that she trusted him…more than he trusted himself.

He stood, and her hand dropped from his shoulder.

He towered over her. He'd intended to appear menacing. To intimidate her into stepping back, but she didn't.

She tilted her head and regarded him with both defiance and a question in her eyes. "Am I—" she began again.

"Yeah, you're right." He would protect her to his last breath. She was his assignment. And he was a fool.

For despite knowing what it felt like before to care about the subject of his mission, to despise himself when he couldn't keep her alive, Dianna Englander had gotten to him.

"Travis," she whispered. Did she step forward to plant her body against his? Or did he move first?

Who the hell cared?

For she was in his arms, and he bent down so that he could cover her lips with his. Hard.

Her hands reached up. He felt her pressing the back of his head, stroking her fingers through his hair.

Holding him so he couldn't end the kiss if he wanted to.

Which he didn't.

Her body moved even closer. She couldn't help but feel his straining erection. Even that didn't make her step back.

She tasted hot and luscious and so female that he ached with wanting her.

If there hadn't been a team of techs down the hall—

Damn! What was he doing? They could walk in at any time, find him fraternizing with his subject. For real, and not just for cover. If he kept his job, he'd never live it down.

He ended the kiss. Or tried to. She held on so it took him a moment longer. A moment of sheer heaven.

He stepped back then, without quite looking her in the

eye. "You don't need to practice our undercover story here, Dianna."

"Really?" He did meet her gaze then, and saw the irony in her expression—though her eyes' heavy-liddedness told him she'd been as affected as him. "I suppose not. The cops down the hall know I don't really lust after you, right?"

"Yeah." He heard the disgruntled note in his tone and gave a wry grin. "Too bad I get caught up in the roles I assume while on a mission. But if you want me to give all that protection you asked for, you have to stop distracting me."

"Of course. So…at the office I pretend I can't keep my hands off you. Around here—" She broke off as a knock sounded on the door.

"Lieutenant, there's something in the kitchen we need to show you," said one of the technicians.

"Sure." He noted the flush rise up Dianna's face. "Around here," he finished for her, "the operative word is vigilance, not cover."

DIANNA, FEARFUL OF what had been found, followed Travis and the investigator down the hall. She watched from the kitchen doorway.

"It's lighter fluid," the guy told him.

She confirmed that she kept some at the top of her pantry. They concluded that it spilled when the shelf was trashed. It probably didn't mean Farley intended to set a fire that night. A conscienceless beast like him would simply have done it.

Good thing, though, that they hadn't decided to show him the lighter fluid a minute earlier, she thought as she continued to watch the team brief Travis on what they'd found.

She had kissed Travis again, when no one was looking. When their surreptitious story of flirtation didn't need to be followed as his cover.

She had reveled in every moment of that kiss. What had she been thinking?

She *hadn't* been thinking. She had just allowed her overwrought emotions to take charge.

He'd admitted that someone under his protection had died. Was that why he was so bossy, so insistent that she follow his commands? Because he feared failing again?

He'd said that other woman—Cassi—had ignored his orders...and died as a result.

Well, Dianna'd had little choice with Brad, for she had intended to stay married to him, especially after she got pregnant. But now, she wouldn't take orders. Not any more. Not Travis's, or anyone else's. Not unless she agreed with them.

But one thing she knew was that she had to avoid kissing Travis, cover or not. She'd been with Brad for two years. They'd been wonderful in some ways, but she'd hated losing herself. She would never get that close again to another man who told her what to do, no matter how well-intentioned his reasons. She had a new life now. And if her failing to follow orders killed her, it would be her own fault, not Travis's.

No, it would be that damned Farley—

"We're done here," the head of the team told Travis.

"Fine," he said. "You got the number for that cleaning crew?" She saw him jot it in a small notebook from his pocket.

When they were alone, he tore the page out and handed it to her. "I hear they come twenty-four hours a day."

"Tomorrow's soon enough," she said. She didn't want to look at the mess any longer. Or think about it. "I suppose you're going to insist on staying here tonight."

"If you are. But there are a lot of nice hotels—"

"No."

"You're right, then. I do insist. Farley would never believe you're lusting after the help if you kick me out now, when he's just scared the living daylights out of you. Besides, even though I'll have a very obvious team outside keeping an eye on things, I have to hang around to watch over you. How else can I redeem myself for past mistakes by getting myself killed while saving your life?"

Startled, she looked up at him. His face was expressionless. But there was a twinkle in his eyes. He was teasing. And yet, she had no doubt that, inside, he meant it.

"You're nuts." She turned to go up the stairs.

But despite how chilled she should have felt after Farley's assaults on her security that day, she felt the warmth of Travis's protection surround her as she headed for bed.

"Okay, Sleeping Beauty. Rise and shine."

Dianna rolled over, groaned as her body reminded her it was bruised, and blinked at the sound of the demanding voice. And then she sat up.

Travis's muscular form was backlighted in her doorway.

"What time is it?" She knew she sounded grumpy, but her room was still dark and she ached.

"Six-thirty." He stepped inside, and she saw that he was, unsurprisingly, dressed in the clothes he'd worn yesterday. She'd heard him shower in the guest bathroom as she lay in bed the night before, making an unsuccessful attempt to sleep.

Especially because she'd pictured Travis naked and twisting in the small enclosure, rubbing his own wet skin everywhere….

"I've made coffee," Travis continued, "but I wasn't able to find enough surviving food or cookware to do breakfast."

"How did you manage coffee?"

"Amazingly, your coffeemaker and a bag of ground beans in the freezer both survived."

"Amazing," she agreed reverently. "But if it's only six-thirty, why are we awake?"

Not that she wasn't already awake. She hadn't slept much. And it wasn't just thoughts of Farley's multiple attacks or even her soreness that had kept her eyes open in the darkness, watching the shadows formed by the nightlight she kept on in the adjoining bathroom.

No, those thoughts kept returning to the knowledge that Travis, the man she was supposed to lust after—*did* lust after—was only a door away.

She imagined a zillion excuses for going down the hall. She could have realistically—genuinely—pleaded fear. Maybe she'd have convinced him that "distracting" him in the middle of the night wasn't a problem.

But she'd have been countering her own principles.

"I take it you're not a morning person," he said.

"I certainly am," she contradicted. "Just not an *early* morning person."

He laughed. "Tell you what. I've got to make some calls. Get dressed and drink your coffee, then we'll figure out the breakfast part. Someplace we can strategize about Farley."

"Okay."

He crossed the room and held the steaming white mug out to her. He looked so damned wide awake, even in the faint light that spilled from her bathroom. He'd probably not had to comb his light brown hair, since he kept it so short. She could see his grin, almost view the teasing twinkle in his blue eyes. "Thanks." She reached out.

Her fingers touched his as he transferred possession of the cup. But he didn't completely let go. He grabbed her other wrist with his hand. "Careful. It's hot." His voice was low, and Dianna wondered for a moment if he was talking about the coffee or his own heated flesh as it caressed her.

"I know." She drew her hand toward herself. The movement brought him closer, too. And closer…

"So you really are Sleeping Beauty?" he asked.

"What do you mean?"

"Well, if I remember my fairy tales, she had to be awakened by a kiss." Before she finished her sharp intake of breath, Travis's mouth was on hers once more.

This time, the kiss was bold but brief, leaving her lips feeling awfully bereft as he backed away.

Only the huskiness of his voice suggested that he might have felt as aroused by the fleeting contact as she was. "Time to get dressed, princess."

FOR HIS PEACE OF MIND, for Dianna's safety, Travis knew he had to keep clear of her that day.

Distraction, hell. The woman was one incomparable actress, the way she'd thrown herself into kissing him yesterday. And those licentious looks she shot his way this morning—well, they mirrored exactly what his own hormones hummed at him, way deep inside.

His cover started out only as a flirtation, but this…this was all-out, no-fooling lust.

"So," he told her after ensconcing her again at her office at Englander Center. "Snail, here, is your employee du jour again. A temporary male secretary of astonishing capability."

Pinkness flowed up the kid's face. He stood military stiff beside Dianna's desk. He wore a dark suit in keeping with the lawyers' expectations in this building, poor guy.

Travis had put on a fresh uniform for his cover, too—a clean pair of jeans and a deep blue T-shirt. He always kept spares in his car. And then, of course, his favorite small gun was loaded and against his ankle, where it belonged.

"Your duties will be simple today," Dianna said lightly. "Just keep me alive and Farley far away."

"Right," Snail mumbled.

"Okay, then, we're straight?" Travis demanded. For breakfast, they had headed for one of the busy family restaurants right there in the civic center area. They'd decided to pretend as if nothing had happened yesterday. If Farley was watching, that should make him mad, for he obviously wanted a rise out of Dianna.

Yes, she was a good actress. And brave.

"We're straight," Dianna agreed. "And now, gentlemen, if you'll excuse me, I have work to do."

"We all do," Travis said. He threw a salute at Snail, then headed for the door.

Of course his first stop was down at Manny's cart. It was the morning rush, and he actually helped the guy sell coffee and doughnuts. When things slowed for a moment, he took out a set of balls and began juggling, just for fun. And so he could put his mind on the day to come. What he had to do.

Fifteen minutes later, his plans had jelled. Filling up a small cart with goodies, he headed into the building.

Chapter Ten

"Just wanted to give you a heads-up, Cal," Travis told Flynn.

Since the security chief didn't have an office, Travis had led him into the community room on the first floor. It was large and as opulent as the building's lobby, with chandeliers dripping crystal over rows of empty red velvet chairs. Looked as if no expense had been spared here to impress the community. Or elsewhere in Englander Center, for that matter.

Travis had turned on the row of lights nearest the stage. He levered himself up near the stage-left edge where the proscenium arch began and sat, jeans-clad legs hanging over as he looked down on the glowering Flynn. It seemed really inefficient for this much space to get so little use, but Travis knew it was supposed to play a key role in next week's anniversary shindig.

Dianna's big bash. The bash that might unearth Farley at last. And get him out of Dianna's life. Way out.

And that would end Travis's connection with the beautiful, warm widow, too.

Damn it.

"What's going on, Lieutenant?" demanded the middle-aged guy with the gut beneath his blue uniform.

"Couple of things happened yesterday you should know about," Travis replied. "One was that Dianna's house was disassembled while she was at work, and some nasty messages left on her answering machine."

"Not good," Flynn said, shaking his puffy, scrawny-haired head as if he regretted what he was hearing. "But nothing I have any control over."

"Nope, but you should know about it. Thing is, there was something that went on in your bailiwick, too."

The guy's uniform seemed suddenly to grow tighter. Or maybe he simply stood straighter. "What?"

Travis described the incident in the parking garage. "See, you need to make sure you have patrols everywhere, especially places Dianna goes. The A-S offices should have someone assigned all the time, and the floor of the garage where Dianna parks her car. Plus—"

"We're not paid enough to put that many men on it." Flynn sounded indignant. "Besides, isn't protecting her *your* job?"

"Sure." Travis wanted to shove the guy right in his smug face—though he had a point. "But wouldn't you like to show the execs who pay your bills how much better you are than the cops?"

"Maybe. But we're doing exactly what we were hired to do."

"And that is…?" As little as they could get away with. But Travis didn't say that.

"We screen people coming in and out. We patrol the building and garage on a schedule, plus do random rounds."

"You haven't added security cameras to record entrances and exits. Any reason why not?"

"We weren't paid to."

It was all Travis could do not to sing along with that

anticipated tune. But the guy was right. A good video system had a high price. Was it worth it here?

Yeah, if it'd catch Farley. Even if the guy had been in the security business, knew the tricks, he'd not be able to knock out surveillance stuff up high but in plain view, wired to avoid tampering. Travis would make sure some high-tech zingers were added fast, even if just temporarily, before the bash next week.

"But with all you've been doing," Travis said, "Farley got by you, at least twice. Why is that?" When Flynn opened his mouth, Travis beat him to the punch. "Yeah, I know, he's gotten past me, too. What do you say we coordinate better, Flynn? Who knows? Maybe that way we'll actually catch the SOB."

THAT MEETING HURT, Travis acknowledged to himself as he pushed the little yellow cart out of the elevator onto the eighth and top floor of the Center. But he'd had to do it. He hadn't wanted to acknowledge that the farce of a security force actually could come in handy. But there were only so many guys assigned here from "L" Platoon, and sometimes being out in the open evoked even more results than all the covert stuff in the world.

He knocked on the first office door. "Goody time," he told the receptionist for the retired judges officed inside, guys who did both mediations and formal courtlike trials.

He described some fake two-for-one coffee and doughnut offer he made up on the spot, the better to get a look at as many people in the place as possible. Only then did he go into his spiel about how ugly that bomb scare had been the other day, and had anyone seen anything suspicious? After all, he was putting together entertainment for the big anniversary celebration next week, and he sure didn't want to bring his performing buddies into a hotbed of danger.

Everyone agreed. But no one had seen anything worth gossiping about either on the day of the bomb scare or otherwise.

He hit all the offices on the floor. The seventh story housed several mock courtrooms, all busy, so he couldn't interrupt. The fifth floor, too. But he visited as many offices as he could.

Nothing useful. But it gave him an excuse to smile into a lot of faces that he studied, looking for Farley.

Didn't find him, though.

He took his time at the sixth-floor offices of A-S. Not that he expected to learn anything new there. But he made it a point to check whether Snail was doing a good job as Dianna's secretary-bodyguard. He was.

Dianna didn't seem too pleased, but at least she was safe. And seeing her was the main reason Travis wasn't in a big hurry to leave….

He talked to Beth. The pretty receptionist was still bent out of shape that he'd shoved his cart by her, burst in on her bosses. Maybe they'd made a stink about it.

"I don't understand why they didn't kick you out," she said, pouting. "They never order that kind of stuff." She looked him square in the face. "What are you really selling them?"

"Love Potion Number Ten." He grinned and pulled a ten-dollar bill from behind her ear. "Better than number nine any day."

Though she laughed, her gaze remained speculative. Was there a reason for her curiosity besides good old bulldog loyalty?

When he finally made it downstairs to the lobby again, he pushed his cart into the little coffee shop, giving a big, friendly grin when its bad-tempered owner Bill Hultman hustled over and tried to shoo him out. The background check Travis had ordered on him had been clean. That didn't mean the guy was perfect, just not caught at anything bad…yet.

Was it show, or did Hultman really think about getting out of his lease by setting a bomb? He got a lot of customers from out on the plaza. What if one was Farley?

"Got a business proposition for you, Bill," Travis said, deflating his pumped-up ire. "I don't just sell food. I represent some entertainers who'll be here next week for the big anniversary celebration. Giving a show attracts a lot more customers." But though his lead-in convinced Hultman to let him question his employees about things they'd heard and seen—ostensibly to make sure Travis didn't lead his buddies astray about their performing gig—no one reported anything amiss.

Not even any crazed customers talking to their boss.

He even spoke with the managers of the bank and the convenience store. The bank had its own security. He made a mental note to have his boss secure copies of their videotapes. He'd let Dianna watch them, see if she recognized Farley.

It was late by then. He'd pretty well wasted the whole day. He checked in again with Snail, made sure Dianna was okay, then headed out to the Van Nuys Police Station. There, he went up to the second floor—actually the third floor, since the fifties-vintage building's basement was really street level. Travis talked to some of the detectives he knew. They'd kept in touch with the Bomb Squad, coordinated with investigators who'd been working the explosion at the redevelopment area downtown, near the Convention Center.

Still a waste of a day. No one knew anything.

Damn.

As Travis helped Manny pack up his stuff for the day, his cell phone rang.

"Lieutenant, it's Snail."

Travis's gut became one huge mass of painful spikes. "What's wrong with Dianna?" He began sprinting inside as he continued to speak.

"Nothing, but she's gone."

"What do you mean? I told you to—"

"To stick with her. Right. Except when she went to the john, and that's what she did. I think. See, she told me she intended to go home with Jeremy Alberts and his little girl, who came here after school. I said I'd come along, and she got mad. So, I told her I'd call you. She told me she'd rather I be the one to tag along, just to wait till she was out of the rest room and we'd catch up with the Alberts. Only—"

"Only she gave you the slip. Damn it, Snail—"

"Yes, sir," said the glum voice at the other end.

"Free!" Dianna whispered as she turned on the lights in the basement of Englander Center.

For now.

Travis would probably have poor Snail's tail for letting her out of his sight, but she couldn't stand it any longer. She hated feeling like this: under a microscope, every second of every hour.

But she'd come spontaneously, telling no one, and made sure she wasn't followed. Even brought a can of mace in her pocket, just in case. She was prepared. Alert.

Of course she'd hate it worse if she had another day like yesterday, where Farley continuously found ways to frighten her.

Later, she would call Travis from the Alberts' and let

him chew her out, stay the night again. That torture—unfulfilled desire—was the worst punishment he could give her, other than handing her over to Farley.

She'd called several subcontractors today to make appointments for them to see this area. She would obtain bids, then A-S would hire the subcontractors to get her children's day-care-playroom started. She'd neglected it long enough.

But was it a totally unachievable dream? This room looked worse each time she visited it. Or maybe removing the trash only called attention to its shabbiness. But surely a new plastering job and bright paint would get rid of the cracks in the walls, and a nice floor with designated play areas, the right staff—it would be wonderful when she finished it.

If she finished it.

If she lived long enough...

Damn! Farley wasn't going to intimidate her like that. Still, she reached for her cell phone. She should call Travis, to avoid being alone. Instead, she took the elevator upstairs.

"Ms. Englander!" Cal Flynn hurried over to her. "Are you by yourself?" He peered behind her into the empty elevator.

"Not anymore. Would you mind walking me to my car?"

"Not at all."

And that gave Dianna an excuse not to call Travis. She'd get in touch with him. Soon.

But for the moment, she'd continue to enjoy her freedom.

Only, as she thanked Cal and headed her little red car down the ramp, she realized she missed her ornery, overbearing bodyguard. Which was all the more reason to request that he send someone else over to watch over her that night.

It most likely wouldn't be poor Snail, after she'd given him the slip. Travis would probably sic someone as sticky as he was on her after that.

She headed her car south, onto Van Nuys Boulevard.

At six in the evening, the civic center was no longer crowded. Most official business was concluded by late afternoon. Since it was winter, the streets were dark, though the streetlights rained soft illumination.

She approached an intersection, realizing at nearly the last moment that the light was already amber, about to turn red. She stepped on the accelerator and made it through, then glanced guiltily to make sure no cop had observed that ungraceful maneuver.

As she looked into the rearview mirror, she noticed that a car had followed her through the intersection—on the red light. "Wow, you've really got guts," she murmured into her empty car.

Except for road noises, only quiet surrounded her, so she turned her radio to a news station.

She scanned the road, slowed for traffic ahead, then glanced into the rearview mirror again to make sure no one was about to thump into her.

That same car was awfully close to her rear bumper.

Just some bad driver, she tried to convince herself. Yet, at the next opportunity, she made a quick right turn without a signal.

So did the car behind her.

Oh, heavens! She couldn't make out the driver in the darkness, or even the car, except that it was a whole lot bigger than her little sports vehicle—a minivan, maybe, or an SUV. Light color.

She made another unheralded maneuver, to further convince herself she was being followed.

She was.

Her heart thumped at triple its normal rate. Tears welled in her eyes but she blinked them away. She didn't dare allow anything to interfere with her vision or any other sense she might use to get herself out of this.

Especially touch. She reached for her cell phone and pushed the button to recall recently phoned numbers. She called Travis.

Only then did she realize the mistake she'd made. She should have stayed on Van Nuys Boulevard, a main thoroughfare. Now, she was on a side street, with fewer cars and dimmer lights.

What was she going to do?

"Dianna?" Thank God! Travis's calm but irritated baritone sounded in her ear, a little tinny due to cell phone static. His caller ID had told him who she was.

"Travis, I'm in trouble. I think it's Farley. I'm in my car, somewhere on Cedros Avenue, I think. I'm being followed." She heard a sob in her voice but got herself back under control. "Where are you? Can you help me?"

If only she'd listened to him. Called him before. If only—

"Yeah, I can help you," he said, just as the car behind her speeded up and pulled alongside her.

She nearly screamed—till she got a good look at the driver.

And then she swore aloud.

The person in the driver's seat of the other car was Travis, his cell phone held to his ear.

He didn't look at all happy.

TRAVIS WASN'T USED to helping kids with homework.

But after giving Dianna the usual chewing out—
stronger this time, since she'd gotten Snail in trouble—
he'd given in to her plea. She'd been on her way to the
Alberts' to help Julie.

He'd followed her there.

Nice place they lived in. Studio City, up in the hills,
behind a security gate and winding, eucalyptus-lined
driveway. There must have been money in real estate
development.

Now, they all sat in a kitchen the size of his Hollywood apartment. Maybe bigger. The table was glass on
wrought-iron, with matching chairs whose seats were
covered with green pillows.

Jeremy, who'd removed his tie and loosened the top
buttons of his white shirt, was reading a stack of mail
that was more than Travis received in a month. His thin
cheeks were sucked in as he scowled at something. Probably a bill. Maybe worrying over them had been what
caused his hair to go gray. He sat across the wide table
from Travis, nearest Dianna. Of course.

Travis had already figured that the guy had the hots
for his employee. Who didn't?

"But I don't care if Indianapolis is the capital of In-
diana," Julie was wailing. She was at Dianna's other
side, where Travis wanted to be. Instead, he sat at Julie's
left.

Poor kid. He hadn't cared, either, at her age.

But then, at her age, he'd tried damned hard to learn
that garbage anyway. He'd always assumed that, if his
grades were good, the latest foster family wouldn't send
him back so fast.

Usually, he'd been wrong.

"Your test is in two days," Dianna said patiently.

She, too, looked more relaxed away from the office—though he could only wish she'd loosen a few buttons of her soft and clingy cream-colored blouse so that he could drool over her soft curves even more....

Of course he could see the blue and green bruising at her neck now, not all hidden by her shoulder-length blond hair. He grimaced as he realized how tight his fist was clenched.

"If you don't study now," Dianna continued, pointing a slender finger toward the page in the textbook, "you won't learn it, and—"

"And let's give the kid a little incentive here," Travis interrupted, drawing his attention back to the little girl with long hair spilling down the back of her knit top. The sooner they got her on the right track, the sooner they'd get out of here. Back to Dianna's place, he figured. She'd had the cleaning crew in, so he doubted he'd convince the stubborn woman to spend the night somewhere else.

Like at his teensy, dingy flat.

"What do you mean, Travis?" Julie asked

"Well, first, you're right. Memorizing fifty states and all their capitals is the pits. It's just names. But what if you plan to visit them someday? That'll make it more interesting."

Julie's young brow furrowed skeptically. "But what's to visit in Indianapolis?" She singsonged the name.

"You gotta be kidding! Ever hear of the Indy 500?"

She shook her head.

"It's only one of the greatest annual car races there is." As the kid's eyes brightened, Travis went on, "Bet you can find out something about each of these towns, though they won't all be fantastic car races. Honolulu,

Hawaii, has the hula, and Juneau, Alaska, has a glacier you can nearly walk up to.''

"Wow!" Julie said, showing her slightly crooked teeth in a large grin.

"Tell you what," Travis said. "You study now for half an hour. When you're done, tell me what you'd like to see in a dozen capitals, and then I'll give you another juggling lesson. And if you ace that test, you and I will spend a whole afternoon together juggling one of these days."

"Yeah!" Julie said, taking the study guide eagerly from the smiling Dianna.

Too bad the kid's father's glare didn't look so happy.

Get over it, Travis thought.

"THAT WAS REALLY NICE of you," Dianna told Travis later, when they were at her house.

She'd known he would suggest that she spend the night somewhere else, even the Alberts', but she wanted to go home. To make sure the cleaning crew had gotten everything.

To assure herself that Farley wasn't in control of her life.

"Yeah, I'm just a nice guy." Travis's sexy leer belied his words. Good thing they were in her living room with the TV turned to the day's news. He leaned back on a comfortable chair, his jeans pulled taut at the thighs as he crossed one leg over the other. The lights were bright, the atmosphere not at all conducive to lustful thoughts.

Otherwise, she just might want to do something about the pulse of desire that shot through her.

"A nice guy who's spending entirely too much time on the job," she observed. "Don't you ever take any R and R?"

"Every day, when I'm juggling," he said. He sounded serious. Maybe he *was* serious.

She certainly didn't find juggling relaxing. Fun, but not relaxing.

"I really enjoyed our lesson," she told him, meaning it. Julie had put in the required study time, and Travis had kept his promise, tutoring her in juggling. He'd invited Dianna to join in, and she'd jumped at the opportunity. Travis hadn't had his usual equipment along, so he'd practiced with tennis balls with Julie, and Dianna had gotten her wish: working with knives. Blunt, safe butter knives from a kitchen drawer, to be sure, but he had assured her that the techniques were the same with the brutal, sharp blades he tossed. Dianna was proud of how well she'd done, but she'd really had to concentrate.

Now, Travis took a swig of the imported beer she had handed him from her refrigerator. Right from the bottle, of course. No wimpy glasses for Lt. Travis Bronson.

She, on the other hand, had decided on a glass of merlot. Probably a bad idea. Didn't alcohol minimize inhibitions? Maybe she would turn her feigned seduction of Travis real that night. It'd be his own fault, since he'd insisted on staying here rather than getting some other member of his team to baby-sit her.

As if she wanted a baby-sitter. And she wasn't exactly a pro at seduction.

But she *did* like the feeling of security it gave her to have someone here, after Farley's last barrage. Particularly Travis. He'd claimed to have been joking about being willing to give his life to protect her, but deep down she knew it was real.

Shuddering as she thought of Brad and how he'd died, she took a sip of her wine. "When did you start juggling?" she asked. Surely that wasn't too personal a question, but she wanted to know more about him. He'd told her very little about himself, except for that poor woman Cassi, whom he'd cared about, and who'd died.

"When I was a kid," he said. "A little younger than Julie."

"Really? Magic tricks, too?"

"Sure."

"Did you go to juggling school, or—"

He laughed aloud. There was an edge to it that she didn't understand. "Nope. I'm self-taught."

"Where did you grow up? Were you—"

"You're full of questions." And he didn't sound inclined to give the answers. She looked into his eyes. There was a remoteness there suddenly that made her feel chilled.

But that neither assuaged her curiosity nor convinced her to give up. "Tell me about your childhood, Travis."

He didn't say anything for a long minute, just studied her with a faraway expression that suggested he wasn't going to say anything. But then he did talk. Casually. As if what he described was normal, pleasant, the childhood every kid wanted.

But it had been hell.

"Not much to say," he began. "I was born here in L.A. My dad was in sales. We were all in a car one day when I was about eight—my dad, mom, older brother and me. A drunk broadsided us. Killed everyone but me, and I was pretty mangled."

Dianna drew in her breath. "Oh, Travis. I'm so sorry. I didn't mean to dredge up—"

He kept going. "I didn't have any other relatives, so after all the surgeries, when I could walk again—more or less—my guardian, the government, threw me into a series of foster homes. Like Julie, I hated it when the kids made fun of me, the way I limped and all. Couldn't beat 'em all up—not then, not till I'd taught myself to fight, though I joined after-school boxing, wrestling and football to get myself into shape whenever I could. Even lost the limp—most of the time. Meantime, I figured I'd entertain them and myself. I learned juggling, card tricks, whatever. Eventually, I joined the Army, and when I got out I went to school, joined the LAPD. That's it—more than you asked for.'' His grin was so brittle that Dianna wanted to wipe it away before his face shattered into a thousand pieces.

She ached for him and the hurt child he once was. She yearned to hold him, to give what small comfort she could. Before she knew what she was doing, she'd crossed the room and sat on his lap. She pulled his head toward her, placed her lips on his. He didn't respond at first, but when she licked his mouth, it opened.

His kiss was hungry, desperate, demanding. Desire surged through her everywhere. One of his hands began to undo her buttons, and all she could do was lean back a little, giving him access. ''Travis,'' she murmured against him.

She didn't recall moving from the chair to the sofa, but she lay there with him on top of her, touching her, kissing her. Her own hands stroked, too, inside his shirt, down the back of his tight jeans, and forward—

As the phone rang.

Dianna froze. Farley. It had to be Farley. Only Farley called her.

Travis was suddenly standing beside her.

''Don't answer,'' she demanded.

''If it's Farley, we may be able to trace it.'' That was why he'd insisted that she leave the ringer on. His breathing was fast, his T-shirt partly raised, exposing the flat belly she had been touching a moment earlier.

But the continued ringing was like a shower of cold water to Dianna.

Travis lifted the receiver and handed it to her, though he kept his head pressed against hers so he could hear, too.

"Hello?" she said, her voice quivering, her body braced in anticipation of that horrible laugh, that mocking voice...

"Dianna, it's Wally."

"Oh. Hi." She pulled back to glance her puzzlement at Travis. Though she spoke often to Jeremy because of Julie, his partner Wally never called her at home.

"Dianna, you have to understand." Something that sounded like desperation pealed from his voice. "I didn't want..." He tapered off.

"What's wrong?" she asked.

"Nothing. Only... Well, nothing I can talk about over the phone. We'll talk tomorrow. First thing in the morning, okay?"

"All right. But, Wally, if you want—"

She realized she was speaking into nothingness, for he had hung up.

"I don't understand," she told Travis. "That didn't sound like him."

"Well, we'll find out what's up in the morning." Travis stood, looming above her. "I'm going to turn in."

The mood between them had obviously been destroyed. Though his handsome, angular face was calm, Dianna sensed a world of whirling emotions behind his cool blue eyes. Was he embarrassed about revealing so much about himself?

She hoped not.

But this night, it wasn't so much lusting after the man who slept one room down from her that kept Dianna awake. No, it was sorrow for the crippled, sad, lonely little boy he had been.

And worrying about what was wrong with Wally.

THEY GOT AN EARLY START in the morning. Dianna glanced in her rearview mirror often on the way to the office, making certain that Travis followed close behind. He accompanied her into the building from the parking lot.

"Let's meet down here at Legal Eats for breakfast in an hour," she told him in the lobby. "You go help Manny set up his cart, and I'll check to see if Wally came in early."

He seldom came in *this* early. But after that cryptic phone call, Dianna figured he was acting out of character anyway.

"No," Travis said. "We'll go up to your offices together."

"But…" No use arguing with him. She turned her back and entered the next elevator car going up.

The office door wasn't locked, and the reception area's lights were on. "Maybe he did come in early," Dianna told Travis.

Noticing that Beth's computer was humming, a green light signifying it was on despite the blank screen, she preceded Travis down the hall.

Wally's office door was shut, so Dianna knocked before pushing it open. "Wally, are you here?" she asked as she strode in. And stopped with a gasp.

He *was* there, his head down on his desk.

"Wally, are you asleep? Did you stay here all night?"

He didn't answer. But he moved, ever so slightly.

And moaned.

"Stay here, Dianna," Travis ordered. She ignored him, approaching her boss and friend.

She saw the knife protruding from his back, then. The blood that had flowed from the wound and all over the chair, the floor.

"Wally!" she shrilled.

He shifted, ever so slightly. She saw his lips move.

She bent so she could hear him.

"Up…set," he said. "Up…set."

"Yes," she said as soothingly as she could, though her heart slapped irregularly within her chest. "Of course you're upset. Just hold on. Please, Wally. We'll get you help."

Another kind of sound emanated from his lips—a gurgle. An expelling of breath.

And Wally said no more.

Chapter Eleven

Travis started making calls the moment he took in the scene at Wally's office. The emergency medical technicians arrived within minutes.

He held Dianna tight while the EMTs worked on Wally, for, stubborn lady that she was, she refused to leave the room.

"He kept saying 'upset, upset.'" She spoke brokenly against Travis's chest. "I couldn't calm him." She swallowed a sob. "I couldn't help him."

"You did what you could," he soothed.

Upset. What had Wally meant by that?

Ignoring the paramedics' exclamations and activity as they continued their frantic ministrations, he glanced around. A wastebasket near Wally's desk was "upset." Papers spilled onto the floor. He wanted to look at them but couldn't let Dianna go. Not now. Not the way she was trembling.

He did, however, pull his cell phone from his pocket and, using his free hand, punched in Snail's cell phone number. "Get over here." He quickly explained the situation. "You need to look for our suspect. Get some patrol officers here to secure the area, and send the SID investigation team on the way, too." He left unsaid that the Robbery-Homicide Division detectives might be needed as well.

"Right."

The EMTs had lifted Wally onto a gurney. IV tubes dangled from a bottle one medic held as they hurried toward the door.

Dianna pulled away from Travis and touched the nearest EMT's arm. "Is he going to be all right?" she asked anxiously.

"Too soon to tell." But the guy met Travis's eye over Dianna's head. That look told Travis everything. There wasn't much hope for Wally. Which made Travis's gut compress as if he'd gotten it caught in a juice squeezer on Manny's cart.

Before they were gone, he got the names of the EMTs so their identities could be entered on the crime-scene log. The investigators would need to keep track of exactly who had been there and when. And taking a few steps from Dianna, he quietly placed a call to Robbery-Homicide.

Wally wasn't Travis's mission, yet he was involved in the assignment. Travis was to protect Dianna while keeping an eye on Englander Center and the people entering and exiting.

He was to find Farley and stop the bastard, before he hurt Dianna or anyone else.

It was another damn mission on which he'd lost someone.

Travis didn't just want to juggle his knives right then. He wanted to use them as weapons.

Maybe on himself.

"But why?" Julie cried as Dianna knelt and took her into her arms. "Uncle Wally never hurt anybody."

Dianna wasn't certain how she had gotten through the day. Now, it was after school, and Jeremy had brought his daughter back to the A-S offices. Because of the continued investigation, Jeremy had to hang around a while longer.

So did Dianna.

"No, sweetheart," Dianna said, murmuring against the child's hair. They were in her office, since it was farthest down the hall and therefore not the center of official activity. "Uncle Wally was a very nice man."

Was. Past tense.

Though he had been alive when the EMTs had taken him out—barely—he had died on the way to the hospital.

Upset. He had been upset. And now it was his survivors' turn to be upset. No, devastated.

For Julie was right. Wally had been a nice man, and he would be missed.

"Why does everyone die?" Julie asked, her broken voice barely a whisper.

Poor kid. She had lost her mother only about a year earlier, and now her mother's brother. It wasn't fair.

"It's difficult, isn't it, honey? That's why we have to live the best we can. And remember the people we lose, and love them always."

"I will." Julie choked and trembled in Dianna's arms.

"Hey, ladies."

Dianna hadn't even noticed her office door opening. She glanced up to find Travis standing there. His face was gaunt, his expression as fierce as she had ever seen it.

But when his dismal blue eyes met hers, they brightened, as if he had forced on a light inside.

"What are you doing here," he asked, "when all the fun is downstairs?"

"Have more performers arrived?" Dianna asked, thanking him with her gaze. Though she did not want to minimize Julie's grief, a distraction would be welcome.

"Yep. There are a lot better jugglers and magicians than me, and—"

Julie pulled away and put her hands on her hips. "No one's better than you, Travis," she contradicted.

"Well, you've got to go see and make up your own mind."

Julie looked at Dianna, who stood beside the child. "Can we, Dianna?" Though tears still glistened in her eyes, hope filled her expression.

Dianna marveled at the resiliency of childhood. "Of course," she said. "And then we can tell Travis which guys he should go take lessons from."

She enjoyed Julie's laugh. And as they passed Travis on the way out of the room, she grasped his large, warm hand in gratitude.

His answering squeeze, along with the way he looked at her, shot a pang of desire ricocheting through her. *Wrong,* she thought. Sex wasn't an answer to grief.

And if she gave in to her urges, she might have a lot more to be sorry about.

BECAUSE TRAVIS HAD told her to wait for Snail to accompany them, Dianna stopped with Julie right outside Englander Center at Manny's pushcart—and within eyesight of Cal Flynn, who had been primed, too, to have his security staff watch over them.

Manny had apparently seen all the emergency activity. "Is everything all right?" the friendly vendor asked, a worried frown creasing his already pleated face even more.

Dianna gave a small, warning shake of her head, and he changed the subject.

"I just got a new kind of ice cream bar," he told Julie. "I need someone to taste it and say if it is good or not." He handed one to the child, who took his question seriously, sampling chocolate and ice cream carefully before expressing her opinion: that it was tasty indeed.

Before Julie finished eating, Travis joined them, along with Flynn. "Looks as if you get Mr. Flynn, here, for company," he said. "There's a call coming in that I have to take, and I can't spare Snail."

He shared a glance with Dianna. She wasn't certain how to interpret it but gathered that the crime-scene investigation was not going well.

"We don't really need—" she began.

"Yeah, you do. Flynn, you're in charge."

Dianna caught the way Travis looked at Cal Flynn, who glared back. Travis must have instructed the resentful security guard on how to do his job.

She didn't really want a watchdog, especially one who probably didn't want to be with her, either. But she was too shaken over Wally's death to argue with Travis just then. Plus, she had to do all she could to distract Julie.

And herself.

For now, that meant cruising the plaza area, watching the entertainment like a regular member of the crowd.

Together, the three of them headed toward the Erwin Street Mall, the wide, outdoor promenade between the parallel courthouses and library, with the police station at the end.

It was about the time that the courts let out, so the area was filled with people. As they wended their way through the thick crowd, Dianna noted that a couple of makeshift stages had been erected along the sides of the mall area, in preparation for the Englander Center anniversary celebration. Most festivities would commence in a few days, but to stir up interest a variety of street performers had already been hired as a noisy and tantalizing appetizer.

At least some, Dianna was sure, were undercover cops like Travis. How had they recruited officers who so easily assumed the roles of street performers? Travis had indicated his platoon of undercover cops was special, encompassing all sorts of unusual skills. And he was right. The performers included a guy making balloon animals and passing them out to kids in the crowd, as well as male and female clowns in full makeup, doing cartwheels and pratfalls on the stages. Some used music, though not loudly in this area of government buildings.

All of Travis's colleagues were multitalented, Dianna thought. As he was.

And the way he turned her on with his sensuous kisses, she suspected she had only gotten a hint of the man's many talents.

"Right, Dianna?" asked Julie, grabbing hold of her hand.

"Sorry, honey," Dianna replied, feeling her face redden as Cal Flynn, too, looked at her quizzically. "I wasn't listening. What did you say?"

Julie's face assumed a long-suffering expression, and her tone held exasperation as she repeated, "I said it would be fun to be one of those guys up on stage, like Travis."

"I'm sure it is," Dianna said. She looked to see what had captured Julie's attention. Though the press of people still surged along the mall, a few had stopped to watch the performances. Julie, Dianna and Cal were in the middle of them, right in front of the nearest stage.

A clown on the low platform was doing tricks with a big, floppy bouquet of artificial flowers that changed color, then turned into a walking stick. He grinned proudly and took an exaggerated bow. Of course the crowd clapped.

"How did he do that?" Julie asked wonderingly.

"Maybe Travis will be able to tell you," Dianna said. "You can ask him later, though magicians don't usually tell their secrets, or even those of their competition."

The clown did a few more tricks with his magical flowers. Then he flopped his huge feet over to a corner of the stage, where he bent way over a microphone and tapped it. The tempo sounded as if he had an exaggerated heartbeat. He spoke into the microphone, too close at first so a huge feedback shrill sliced at Dianna's brain. Everyone else's, too, judging from the agonized expressions as people covered their ears with their hands.

"Music to my ears," said the clown in a yuk-yuk tone. "Now, I need a volunteer to help me, right up here." He bent and swept his arm about the stage. A few people waved their hands, including an enthusiastic Julie. But when the clown scanned them, his eyes lit on Dianna. "This lovely lady right here." He pointed one very white finger right at Dianna.

Dianna met Cal's gaze.

He shrugged. "Do it if you want. There's too much going on here for your buddy to try anything."

Just in case, Dianna looked more closely at the clown. Of course the guy wore a lot of makeup, but the shape of his face was too full, his body too slight and short for him to be Farley in disguise.

There was a large crowd around. The clown was in plain sight. What harm could it do for her to play along?

Especially when Julie was tugging at her hand, urging her onto the stage. "Do it, Dianna. Go up there. He wants you."

"All right." She wended her way around to the side of the stage and walked up the makeshift steps.

"What do you want me to do?" she asked the clown.

For the next few minutes, Dianna laughed with the crowd below the stage as she was the brunt of the clown's tricks—unable to open the stick into a bouquet until he tapped her lightly on the shoulder. Opening her mouth at his request, only to have him appear to extract a series of hardboiled eggs.

Fun stuff.

Dianna got into the act, bantering along with him.

She glanced down and gave Julie a wink. Only then did she notice Travis stood beside Flynn and the child. Why was he there instead of at the crime scene?

She had no time to ponder that, for the clown started to juggle a couple of medium-sized balls, tossing them slowly at first. "Here, catch." He threw one toward Dianna, and she caught it. It had the feel of a water balloon. "Don't be selfish. Throw it back."

She complied but said, "I think you've got the wrong person for this. There are some real jugglers around who—"

"Oh, no. I've definitely got the right person." His voice, not fed into the microphone, was suddenly hard, no humor in it at all. And then he pulled a larger ball from somewhere inside his voluminous clothes and lobbed it at Dianna. Fast. Right toward her face.

Instinctively, she raised her hands to shield herself.

She felt the missile hit her with a force she hadn't anticipated.

With a loud pop, it exploded.

Pain rocked through Dianna, even as she felt wetness. She looked down and found herself covered in red dampness. Blood.

Only vaguely aware of the screams and panic around her, she slid to the stage.

Chapter Twelve

Travis leaped onto the stage. "Stay there," he commanded the shrieking Julie. "Dianna will be fine."

He hoped. And he wanted more than he wanted to breathe to check on her. But he couldn't do that yet.

Not without making sure that Farley, the SOB who'd hurt her, wasn't about to do something even worse—to her or to the onlookers. Like explode another, bigger bomb, or do something else to finish Dianna off…assuming she was still alive.

"Damn you," Travis muttered at the bastard he intended to subdue as painfully as possible. He shouldn't have trusted Flynn to keep her safe. If he'd been there, he wouldn't have let her on stage, an easy target for anyone hiding in the crowd to see.

Only it wasn't someone in the crowd who'd harmed her. Farley had been brazen enough to perform in front of everyone, to leave himself open to capture….

Strange. Farley wasn't moving. He looked frozen as he stared down at the limp heap upon the platform that was Dianna.

Travis forced himself not to stare at her, too. So much blood…

"Call 9-1-1," he cried generally into the panicking crowd as he grabbed the clown and wrestled him down onto his stomach.

"I didn't mean it," his unresisting captive said over and over.

"Yeah," Travis said, cuffing the guy's bony wrists behind his back. "Like you didn't mean to kill Wally."

"What? I didn't kill anyone!"

A couple of Travis's platoon members who'd been working the crowd undercover leapt onto the stage. "Take care of him," Travis commanded as the two cops pulled the guy none too gently to his feet.

Then Travis bent over Dianna. He almost sank to his knees in relief, for she was sitting up. Julie, who'd not listened to him, knelt beside her.

"It's okay, honey," Dianna said to Julie. "I'm fine."

Sure she was, with dripping blood turning her soft blond hair into a congealing red mass, her hands raw and...

He didn't smell the metallic stench of blood. And the color of the thick ooze on her and all over the stage, though close to the redness of blood, was a bit too bright.

"Are you hurt?" he demanded anyway, too roughly. He wasn't about to believe she was unharmed. Not with the way his gut had been eviscerated by the thought that he'd lost her.

He'd failed another person he was supposed to protect. And not just any person.

Dianna.

"I... I think it was just a balloon full of red paint, and it exploded," she said. She looked up, her expression almost serene as she made a valiant effort to appear reassuring. But her blue eyes were huge and terrified.

"Yeah," he agreed. "Looks that way."

He reached down, intending only to help her to her feet. But he couldn't help it. He pulled her tightly into his arms and held her against him.

"You'll get paint on you," she protested, but not too strongly, for she held onto him as if she'd been tossed from the roof of Englander Center and he held the only rope that could save her.

As if.

She was hanging onto the wrong lifeline, if she was relying on him. But he couldn't bring himself to let her go. Not when she felt so good—so *alive*—in his arms.

Besides, he told himself, he was helping to restore his cover. He was supposed to be a street performer, not a cop who'd go after the bad guys. But part of that cover was that he was trying his damnedest to seduce Dianna so she'd hire his buddies for the anniversary festivities.

Since most performers were already on board, he could be continuing the seduction for hedonistic reasons. Why not? She was a pretty lady. He was a red-blooded man. End of cover story.

Except that the red blood had been paint…this time. And it had wound up all over Dianna.

It had been his fault. Though the call from his boss, Captain Hayden Lee, had been important, they could have talked later. He shouldn't have been stupid enough to trust Flynn to keep her safe. The fool had let her up on stage.

Had indirectly let Farley get to her.

With a growl of fury, he gently pulled away from her.

"Glad you're okay," he said, barely sparing a glance for the red paint now smeared on his dark T-shirt and jeans. "I need to talk to our friend with the exploding paint balloon."

He motioned to Snail, who had joined them. He must have been summoned when word of what had happened had circulated at the crime scene in Englander Center.

"Keep close watch on her," Travis told him. Unlike Flynn, he could trust Snail. He'd handpicked the guy to be on his platoon.

The clown had been led by the arresting officers along the promenade to the Van Nuys Police Station. Convenient. As one of the primary LAPD stations in The Valley, it had more than just a series of holding tanks. It actually held a jail.

The clown was already in the compact booking area, his vital information being fed into the computer, when Travis caught up with him.

"My name really is John Smith," the guy whined to the officer questioning him. "I'm not in your system because I've never been arrested. It was a joke, man. Just a joke."

"Yeah, funny," Travis said, towering over the guy, who sat in a chair. He looked grotesque, as sweat had caused his clown makeup to run in ruts down his face. "You think blowing up a member of your audience is a big laugh, do you?"

"No, of course not. But the guy who gave me that ball described that lady, said he was her boyfriend and he wanted to play a trick on her. Gave me twenty bucks to say what he told me, then throw the ball like that. 'Course I knew it'd make some noise and mess up her outfit, but I didn't now she'd get so scared she'd faint. Was it because the paint looked like blood?''

''Yeah, something like that,'' Travis said. He wasn't about to give this guy the whole story.

And he was very much afraid this John Smith was telling the truth. They'd know more after his prints were taken and that ugly, running makeup was removed.

But Travis was all but certain that this was not Glen Farley. He had gotten away again.

GLEN FARLEY LAUGHED.

He covered his mouth with a ratty sleeve and turned the sound into a cough. The damn denim jacket he wore smelled of cigarettes, and he didn't smoke. How ironic that the guy he'd lifted it from at the restaurant had left it untended when he'd gone out for a couple of drags. *Finders, keepers.*

Farley stood in the middle of the mall's jabbering crowd that had fled the stage when the balloon filled with paint came apart. Nice touch, adding one of those poppers like kids used at New Year's and the Fourth of July. Made it sound like a small explosion. The people around wouldn't recognize him for the genius he was. They wouldn't recognize him at all.

But he wouldn't laugh among them. He didn't want anyone to remember some crazy guy in their midst who laughed when everyone else was crying.

No, for the police would be asking for people to step forward with anything that would lead to apprehension of the nut who'd played such a nasty trick.

Fools. Sure, they thought him insane. That was part of his plan.

It was almost cool here, in the shadow of the puny library branch in the Van Nuys Civic Center. But the body heat of all the people surrounding him made him itch.

Too bad it hadn't been a real bomb. This time.

This time, no one had gotten hurt. But he'd scared that bitch Dianna Englander again. She deserved it, damn her.

Almost unconsciously, he again fingered the scab that ran down the side of his face, thanks to the key she'd cut him with. Good thing he knew how to use stage makeup. No one who looked at him knew it was there. But *he* knew it.

The crowd began to disperse. No wonder. There wasn't much left to see, since the cops had stopped the rest of the guys and gals from doing tricks on those stupid little stages. And the one Dianna had been on was surrounded by yellow crime scene tape.

She should be grateful to him. She'd stayed alive more than two years after that hypocrite of a husband of hers had sucked in the shots Farley had fired. Once, he'd only wanted to keep on scaring her. He'd planned, then, to let her live. Until he'd been given a nice, lucrative motive otherwise.

So, her reprieve was nearly over. He wanted her to know it.

That was why he'd slipped that ridiculous clown a twenty, along with the paint balloon and instructions about how to spot Dianna and, then, what to do with her.

He'd had different makeup on then. It had made him

look thirty years older. And not a clown. Definitely not a clown.

Oh, how he loved disguises!

Though they might suspect who'd set Dianna up this time, they wouldn't have an accurate description of him.

Not many people besides Dianna knew what he looked like.

Wally Sellers had known. He'd seen him.

Killing Wally had been a stroke of genius.

But Wally's death wasn't the end of it. Not by a long shot.

Farley laughed aloud again once more. Feeling eyes on him, he sobered damn quick and aimed his most bite-me glare at a fat lady who stared at him, pushed against him in the crowd.

She turned away fast. Probably would remember him. But maybe he'd scared her enough that she'd keep it to herself.

If not, so what?

Not even the feds had been able to find him before, thanks to his ingenuity and enterprise.

And now Dianna had her own personalized watch-dogs. Undercover? Not hardly.

He had his sources.

No one, not Dianna and certainly not the local cops, would be able to stop him now.

TRAVIS HELD Dianna tightly at his side as they strolled toward Englander Center. She snugged against him, as if she belonged there. Her soft curves meshed all too well with the lines of his body. It felt good. Too good.

He'd have liked to step up the pace so he could let

go of her. Fast. Before he considered making it even more of a habit. But they had to keep it slow, for, as she leaned on him for support, she was wobbly.

So was he, though he wouldn't let on how he was consciously fighting his limp. When he let emotions get the better of him, his weak leg always gimped up on him.

Emotional? Hell, he was furious. He should take a lesson from Dianna, one brave lady. She kept her chin up despite the streaks of paint on it and on her cheeks. Her eyes stayed straight ahead, except when she looked down at Julie Alberts, who held her hand on the other side.

He felt proud of her. *As if you have a right to, Dumbo.*

"You're sure your friend didn't mind your taking this shirt?" Dianna asked him.

He'd wrapped her in an oversized San Diego Chargers sweatshirt lifted from one of the guys in his platoon. It covered most of the red paint spattered all over her nice beige pantsuit.

Didn't help to cover the blotches on her face that he hadn't been able to wipe away with tissues, nor the garish streaks in her light hair.

Even with all that, her femininity showed through.

"Nah, he didn't mind," Travis replied to her question. Didn't have a choice. Travis had made handing it over an order.

He'd buy it from the guy, though, since the red paint was unlikely to come out.

A couple of teens in baggy pants turned to look at Dianna. Travis stared them down, and they backed off. He had an urge to challenge them anyway but swallowed it. Their curiosity was normal, under these bizarre circumstances.

Besides, it was Farley he wanted to squash. Now.

They reached the sidewalk outside the Center. Manny, who'd been serving a kid a frozen fruit bar, hurried over. "What happened?" he asked. "Are you all right, Dianna?"

"Sure, but boy, is my face red," she quipped.

Travis laughed with the others. Almost without thinking, he hugged her closer. She looked up at him, gratitude—and something else—shining in her eyes.

He didn't want to identify that other thing, for if it was desire, it just might collide with his own and create an explosion neither of them wanted.

One that would do more to them than loosen a little paint.

Bad idea.

They were right outside Englander Center now. Travis could see the security guys inside. Cal Flynn wasn't with them. He was still being questioned by police about what he saw. Which was undoubtedly zilch. The guy could have been asleep and done a better job of protecting Dianna.

Not that Travis had done any better.

Swallowing his self-disgust, he nevertheless released Dianna from his grip. "Take Julie and go up to your office," he said. He pretended not to see the hurt in her eyes as she reacted to his gruffness. Still, more gently, he added, "Soon as I check on what the techs learned today about the…about Wally Sellers, I'll join you."

"No need," she said, though the rough way she swallowed told him that returning to the scene of that crime would be hard on her. Especially after the sneaky way she'd been attacked. "I have to clean up," she continued. "Julie can help. I'll be fine."

"Yeah," he agreed. "You will. I'll see to it."

TRAVIS WASN'T about to follow Dianna into the ladies' room, no matter how much he wanted to attach himself to her. So, while she cleaned up, he walked into what was left of Wally Sellers' office and surveyed the scene.

The techs had put it back, more or less, though he could still see a dusting of black fingerprint powder on a lot of surfaces. And there were a few things missing, like the area rug beneath the desk, some stacks of paper on top of it...most stuff that had probably absorbed Wally's blood.

"What happened to Dianna?" Jeremy Alberts huffed into the room and glared at Travis. How could he stand having his tie so tight at his neck? It made his white shirt collar look stiff and uncomfortable, too. "Beth told me that when you all came through the reception area, Dianna looked as if she was covered in blood, but she claimed it was paint and she should have ducked. What's that about, Bronson?"

Jeremy's reaction was even more proof that his interest in Dianna was more than a boss's. More than avuncular. Probably a lot more than being in the market for a brand new mom for Julie.

He wanted *her*

Join the club. The developer was probably more Dianna's type, though. An executive who didn't work the streets or get his hands dirty. As a building developer, all he'd do was supervise the grunts who did the construction.

A better match for the widow of a U.S. Representative than a juggling cop who too often bungled missions involving keeping a subject safe. Like Dianna.

Jeremy, glaring, obviously expected an answer. Travis figured he owed the man that. He described what he'd found when he reached the plaza, saw Jeremy's prize security chief twiddling his thumbs while Dianna played into Farley's hands on stage. The way the fall-guy clown threw the balloon at her, the way it exploded and showered her with red paint. Travis had bought the performer's story, though he would convict the guy of terminal stupidity for agreeing to play such an ugly joke for twenty bucks.

"I'd suggest you fire Flynn, get his butt out of here," Travis concluded. "I told him to keep an eye on Dianna, and look what happened."

"Would you have done any better, Bronson? Would you have prevented her from going up on that stage?"

Hell yes, Travis was about to say, when a sweetly feminine, but highly determined voice rang out from behind him.

"Of course not," Dianna said. "It was my decision, not Flynn's or Travis's or even Julie's." She smiled down at the child who stood beside her, obviously absorbing every word. Most of the red paint was gone from her face and hair, though she still wore the sweatshirt, over darker slacks than she'd been wearing before.

Alberts was going to have one heck of a time with his daughter as she got older, for the kid clearly was looking up to Dianna as a role model. A damn fine role model, in most ways. But one with a mind of her own, no matter what the circumstances.

No matter what the danger... He swallowed the demands that sprang to his lips. Instead, he said, "You're right, Dianna. But Flynn and I have something in common. We want to make sure you're safe. And for us to do our jobs, we really need for you to cooperate. Got it?" He looked at her long and hard.

Her eyes, that stunning shade of cool blue, seemed to take on an even more determined expression. "You seem to forget—" she began.

"He forgot to say please," piped in Julie.

Travis glared at the impishly grinning child.

"That's right," Dianna said. She, too, smiled. "Say please, Travis."

Saying "please" wasn't in his job description. Still, if it got what he wanted... "Please," he muttered. Damn, that hurt.

"Pretty please with sugar on it," prompted Julie. "Don't press your luck, kid," Travis growled. But when he glimpsed the challenge in Dianna's raised eyebrows, he gave in. "Pretty please with sugar on it. Now, let's go into your office and talk strategy for tonight."

Chapter Thirteen

Standing once more outside Englander Center later that day, Dianna was relieved that Travis insisted he would accompany her home that night. She didn't want to be alone. Not after all that had happened that day.

Poor Wally. *Upset...upset.* His voice moaned over and over in her mind. How could A-S Development continue without the man who had tempered Jeremy Alberts' daunting perfectionism?

For once, she was glad when Travis issued commands that brooked no resistance. She *wasn't* to do anything on her own. He *was* going to hang out with her. And, in the interest of keeping his damned cover viable, he made it a point, before they left Englander Center, to juggle beside Manny's cart as she watched.

"Fare to keep you awake and alive," read Manny's sign. It took on a whole new meaning now. Wally was *not* alive. And she would be awake all night thinking about him.

Travis was magnificent as he twirled four lethal-looking knives and snatched their hilts from the air, his blue eyes dark with concentration. He wore his usual uniform of a snug Cart à la Carte T-shirt over even more snug jeans, and she watched his biceps flex as he tossed and caught the daggers.

The crowd behind Dianna oohed, aahed and gasped at his every movement, and no wonder. What he did was dangerous. *He* seemed dangerous, particularly when he glanced away from his spinning blades and grinned so devilishly at his audience.

Bill Hultman from Legal Eats was in the crowd, scowling. He didn't look impressed. In fact, he appeared to Dianna to be willing Travis to miss and let one of those blades stab into him.

That didn't happen, thank heavens. And when Travis finished, he laid the knives on the cart, then grabbed Dianna and gave her a big kiss.

It's part of his act, she reminded herself as her knees wobbled and she hung onto his hard body for support. She was supposed to play the part of a woman in the throes of seduction so it wouldn't look odd for this street performer to accompany her home.

Play the part? Heck, she only wished that Travis *was* about to seduce her. She had never before met a man who sent desire charging through her like a flash fire the way he did—not even Brad. Maybe, if she actually satisfied her lust with Travis once, she'd get over wanting him so much.

More likely, she'd find making love with him addictive.

"Ready to go home?" he asked, loudly enough that people around could hear. His cover was secure for that night.

And her reputation as a cool, professional manager? Shot to smithereens. She had no idea how she would regain it, with Bill Hultman or anyone, when this was over. If it ever was over…

"Sure," she told him, making her voice sound as turned-on as she could. Which, basking under Travis's sexy gaze, was pretty turned-on. "Let's go."

IT WAS ALL Travis could do that night to shoo Dianna into her bedroom…alone.

He left the door ajar in the room next to hers as he removed his gun from its holster and stripped for bed. He heard her moving around, the sound of the shower in the adjoining master bath. Imagined her under the spray.

He growled aloud and yanked the covers down. Not that he would sleep. And it wasn't just watchfulness that would keep him awake.

Sure, seeming to seduce Dianna was part of his cover. But he wanted her. Really wanted her.

And couldn't have her, for though she had responded to his kiss in the plaza, had pretended she had the hots for him, too, it was part of the act.

If she were really interested… He still couldn't do a damned thing about it, for she was under his protection, and she was much too vulnerable.

A friend of hers had been murdered that day, and she had found him, dying. Then she'd had a scare of her own. All of that while she still wore bruises from her earlier attack.

He flicked off the lamp beside the bed. Wearing only his boxers, he pushed the pillows against the headboard and leaned back against them, reaching between the mattress and springs to make sure his gun was right where he needed it.

A light spilled from beneath Dianna's door into the hall outside. He imagined the illumination growing brighter as she shoved open the door and came into the hall. Into his room. Wearing nothing at all…

"Dumbo," he muttered aloud as the light in the hallway went out.

FOR THE NEXT FIVE DAYS, Dianna waited anxiously for the next shoe to drop.

Where was Farley? she wondered for the umpteenth time one morning as she sat at her desk. Her hands held the press release she was about to distribute about the Englander Center's first anniversary gala, but her eyes didn't really see the page.

Why hadn't Farley done anything else? Was he waiting for the birthday celebration? Jeremy still refused to postpone it.

Dianna took a sip of coffee from the blue ceramic mug she lifted from her nearly empty desk. It tasted bitter. Chilly.

Mirroring the way she felt.

Farley might be lying low because he'd murdered Wally. Not that he'd suddenly developed a conscience. But the police weren't shy about conducting their investigation. They were all over the Center, still asking questions, searching for clues that would bring the murderer in.

They hadn't found Farley.

The cops didn't discuss the case with her, of course. But she could tell from Travis's irritability that not much useful had happened.

"Where are you, you miserable killer?" she demanded as she stared into the impenetrable brown liquid in her cup.

"What's that?"

Startled, she looked up.

Travis had spoken from her office door. His T-shirt that day was a brilliant blue that brought out the brightness of his eyes. Not to mention the breadth of his muscular chest. "Talking to yourself?"

She felt a warm flush inch up her face. "Just reading my promotional copy aloud," she fibbed.

"Fair enough. So, with your promotional copy to keep you company, you don't mind if I go downstairs and juggle a little?"

"Not at all." Of course, the image of him pumping knives turned the heat suffusing her face up a few degrees—not to mention the flame that was continuously lit inside her every time he was around.

Especially at night, every night since Wally's death.

In keeping with his cover, Travis went home with her. But because his presence was simply that—a cover so he could watch for Farley and keep her safe—he merely watched TV with her and gave her an occasional juggling lesson. He'd allowed her to graduate to more potent knives—only one at first, from his box of prized juggling utensils. And he always left her at her bedroom door. Each night, she took an icy shower. For he had been a perfect gentleman. Damn it.

Irritation made her peevish. "Is juggling like twiddling your thumbs? It looks as if you're just biding your time."

His wide jaw tightened. "I am. As I keep close watch for anything—or anyone—suspicious."

"Don't you think by now that Farley's on to you?"

"Could be. I'm also on to him. And I'll get him."

Sure you will, Dianna thought, but kept the sarcasm to herself. It was only her own taut, edgy nerves that made her so cynical anyway. They *would* get Farley. They had to.

But could they do it before he harmed anyone else?

"You'll stay here till I get back," he said, not making it a question. "Snail will hang out in the reception room to keep an eye on things. Beth's making that assignment easy on him."

Dianna had also noticed that the A-S receptionist and the youthful undercover cop had a flirtation going.

Maybe theirs, at least, would come to something....

"Fine," she snapped, then eased up. She smiled at Travis. "Is it appropriate to tell a juggler to 'break a leg'?"

"As long as you don't tell him to break an arm," he riposted with a grin so sexy it made her toes curl. He saluted crisply with one of those sinewy arms, then left.

You'll stay here until I get back. With a sigh, Dianna replayed his command in her mind. Not hardly, she thought.

There was someplace she needed to go.

Not that she'd be foolish about it.

When enough time had passed to be sure Travis had left the suite, she grabbed her purse and headed into the hall. Jeremy strode by as Dianna passed the closed door to Wally's office.

Their eyes met. "How are you doing, Dianna?" The throatiness in her boss's voice hadn't been there last week. Though he didn't express his emotions aloud, he obviously grieved deeply for his partner and friend.

"Okay." It wasn't a lie. She was doing *okay,* but she was certainly not doing *well.* "And you?"

"Surviving." He added hesitantly, "Would you have dinner with me one evening?" He must have sensed her hesitation, for he added, "Julie, too, of course. She's not taking Wally's death well at all."

"I'd love to join you both," Dianna said. Poor Julie.

Poor all of them…

Jeremy headed for his office, and Dianna continued toward the reception area.

Her ubiquitous shadow Snail was there, of course, sitting on the edge of the desk and grinning sappily at Beth. The A-S Development receptionist, an expert at flirtation, had turned all her wiles on the undercover cop. Snail didn't stand a chance.

Dianna rescued him. "Snail, I need to go somewhere."

His posture straightened. "I'll go with you," he said.

"I figured." Dianna didn't look at Beth. Bad enough that she'd been subject to such frustration for the last week. She didn't want to see it mirrored in someone else's eyes.

"What is this place?" Snail asked.

"A children's day-care center." Dianna flicked on some extra basement lights. She had called more subcontractors who could do this kind of work, and in a week or two, after the anniversary celebration was over, she'd start getting bids to convert this dingy, decrepit room into a cheerful, fun one. The need remained for a safe place for kids to be while their parents negotiated in the Center's alternate dispute resolution facilities.

The operative word was *safe*. Would she feel safe putting kids here before Farley was caught?

No. But that didn't mean she couldn't get her plans underway. And once the anniversary bash was over, she'd have more time to devote to it.

"A day-care center? If you say so." Snail sounded dubious. "Look, Dianna, it's awful isolated down here. If Travis knew where we were, he'd fire me—after kicking my butt but good."

"He doesn't have to know." She reached into her purse for a pad of paper and the retractable measuring tape she'd tossed into it. Instead, her fingers touched her cell phone, so she kept searching. "I need to take some measurements since one of the subcontractors I've called—"

She gasped aloud as the lights went out.

"You all right, Dian—?" Snail's shrill voice ceased abruptly, as she heard a heavy thud.

Frightened, she grabbed in the direction of the young cop—just as something stiff and huge and smelling like death was thrown over her.

It pitched her to the floor. "Snail!" she tried to call as her knees struck concrete, followed by her outstretched hands.

In a moment, she lay flat on her face beneath it, unable to breathe, as a muffled but haunting cackle assailed her.

TRAVIS HAD LEARNED, after many years of experience, to trust his gut. Today, it told him things had been too quiet too long.

He didn't find juggling balls relaxing, let alone knives. With a growl, he told Manny he had to go. He headed up the stairs, not the too-slow elevator, to the sixth floor. To Dianna.

His unfulfilled need for the beautiful woman so beyond his league could be what caused his damned gut to rib him as it did. After all, every organ in his body had taken to teasing the part of him that stood at attention every time Dianna was around. Even when she wasn't around. Like at night, when she was in the next room. As far removed from him as if they were in different states.

He burst through the A-S Development door, ready to

rag on Snail for flirting with the receptionist. He had to take this mood out on someone.

Only Snail wasn't there. "Where is he?" he barked at Beth.

The receptionist, who was on the phone, raised one finger signifying she wanted him to wait a minute. He didn't have a minute. "Where—" he began again.

"Excuse me a second," she said into the phone. "They're gone."

"*They*'re gone?" Travis roared. "Where?"

"The basement, I think. I got Dianna a subcontractor's number before, and that usually means—"

Travis didn't wait for the rest of the explanation. He raced once more for the stairwell—just as his cell phone rang.

"Bronson," he barked into it.

"Travis." The voice was weak, muffled. "It's Dianna. Please help."

"WHAT THE HELL were you thinking, Snail?" Travis demanded.

His subordinate sat on the floor, looking dazedly up at him in the dirty yellow light of the basement. Soot smudged his pale cheeks, and he held one side of his head with his hand.

"Don't yell at him," Dianna demanded. "He's hurt." She stood beside Travis now. When he'd gotten down there, gun drawn, and turned on the lights, she'd been nowhere to be seen.

Until he'd noticed the huge black tarp covering the floor begin to move. Covering whoever stirred beneath it with his weapon, he'd yanked it up.

Dianna had been facedown on the floor. His heart had

nearly stopped—until he reminded himself she was moving.

Only then did he stoop beside her and help her up.

"He could have been hurt a lot worse," he said to her now. "You, too."

"I...I know. And I was surprised my cell phone worked down here." Her voice quivered. He glanced at her. She gnawed on her bottom lip, and tears glistened in her eyes as she leaned heavily against the filthy, cracked wall.

If she started crying now, he'd hate himself even worse.

He could have lost her....

He could have lost another person he was assigned to protect, he reminded himself.

"I don't suppose you saw who it was." He forced himself to talk quietly.

"No," she said, "but I heard him. It was Farley. He was laughing. It was a game to him. Just a game. He hurt Snail, smothered me, and—" Her voice rose until she sounded near hysteria.

"It's okay." Travis pulled her against him. She shook all over, and he held her tight, trying to soothe her even as his body responded to her closeness. He ignored his inappropriate response.

"It's not okay," she whispered brokenly as she regained control. "He could have killed Snail."

And you. Travis didn't voice that thought for fear of frightening her even more. Instead, he grasped her tighter. "It won't happen again," he promised.

"But—"

"It won't happen again." But his repetition didn't make it so. His resolve did. For he would not put anyone else in the position Snail had been in before.

It was his job to keep Dianna safe.

And he would.

SHE WAS ALIVE.

At home that night, lying in her bed beneath the sheets scented with familiar laundry soap, in her familiar sleek satin nightgown, Dianna could think of little beyond how it had felt lying beneath that stinking tarpaulin, knowing Farley was there laughing at her. Laughing because she was in his control.

He could have killed her.

He hadn't. She was alive.

Why? So he could taunt her further? Toy with her, until he decided it was her time?

No!

She despised controlling men. She'd hated that about her own otherwise dear husband.

And yet…when Travis told her what to do, even if she didn't like it, she knew it was with one goal in mind: his mission. And that meant keeping her safe.

Travis. He was there. In her house. He had vowed he would not trust anyone else to take care of her. That he would become as close to her skin as her own underwear…

The image had driven her nuts with desire. Maybe tonight, she'd thought.

And yet, when they had gotten here, to her house, nothing had changed. Once again, he'd given her a juggling lesson at her insistence—but she'd been too shaky to do any good. And Travis had remained the perfect gentleman….

Screw him.

Oh, yes. That was exactly what she wanted. She was alive. She needed to feel alive.

Shuddering, praying she wouldn't regret this in the morning, she threw off her covers—even as the door to her bedroom opened. She could tell in the faint glow from the tiny nightlight she had left on in her bathroom.

"Travis?" she whispered.

"Just want to make sure you're all right," he said. The huskiness to his voice told her what she needed to know. He wanted her, too. Even if he'd promised himself to remain the perfect gentleman.

"I'm not all right."

"What's wrong?" The next moment, he was sitting on the side of her bed. "Tell me."

"Only this," she said, reaching for him.

She felt him flinch as she put her arms around him. But when her lips found his, he didn't hold back.

He tasted of the yearning that caused aches inside her that she hadn't felt in years. Had *never* felt, for there was a promise, as he deepened the kiss, of passion yet unawakened deep within her.

"Travis," she whispered against him, only to feel his tongue capture her words, her mouth, her breath.

He eased her back gently onto the bed, settling himself on top of her. She felt the stretchy fabric of his T-shirt against her bare arms. His slim jeans scratching at her legs. His stiffening hardness...

He didn't move. She heard his uneven breathing as he attempted to gain control.

She didn't want his control. Not any more. She wanted *him*.

"This isn't right, Dianna." His voice was low, an agony of reserve.

"It's very right. I'm not asking for forever. I just need to feel alive right now."

She moved slightly, out from beneath him. She used

the opportunity to reach down and maneuver herself out of her silky nightgown, then grabbed for his clothes, the barrier that kept them from being skin-on-skin.

Would he still argue with her? No. Worse. He moved away, and she sighed. Surely he wouldn't just leave.

But, no. She could see in the dimness that he was stripping away his clothing. In a moment, he was back with her.

She gasped at the feel of his hard chest against the sensitivity of her straining nipples. And then his hands were on her. Gently. Stroking. ''Travis,'' she sighed, as his lips closed over one of her aching breasts.

She moved her fingertips over his back, then down the tautness of his buttocks. She squeezed gently, reveling in his quick intake of breath as she moved her hands more determinedly to his front. She smiled against his mouth as she reached his erection.

With a growl, he rolled her onto her back. His mouth moved over every inch of her until she thought she would cry out for wanting him. Maybe she did cry out, for she lost coherency.

He didn't, though, for he moved away for a brief eternity. ''Travis?'' she moaned, then heard a rustling as he found his jeans on the floor. He had come prepared, and she smiled at this man whose focus, no matter what he did, was on protecting her.

She stopped smiling as he positioned himself, ready to thrust inside her. He stopped. ''Please,'' she whispered.

She didn't have to beg further, for in moments, he was inside her, rocking gently at first, then thrusting as she gasped, then called his name as he soon sent her into a frenzy of need that crescendoed and spiraled her over the top, even as he cried out in a shout of release.

BAD IDEA, Travis told himself later as he lay in Dianna's bed, holding her in his arms. But he didn't convince himself.

She felt damned good against him still. Even when he was too tired to do more than clasp her while she slept.

A sense of calm came over him. He'd promised himself, and her, that he would take care of her. Protect her. To do that, he had to be with her.

He couldn't get much closer to her than this.

She stirred against him. "Travis?" she murmured sleepily. Nothing sexy about that, yet he began to throb once more. And grow hard.

"Go back to sleep," he whispered. But her hands did not seem sleepy at all as they ranged over him. He heard her intake of breath, then her dreamy laugh as she found how much he wanted her again.

"I think I need to be relaxed again," she said.

What could he do but oblige her?

Chapter Fourteen

Dianna's eyes popped open.

Her head still on her soft pillow, she found herself staring into Travis's slow grin. She grinned back.

"Good morning," she whispered. But as he reached for her, she remembered what day it was. "We don't have time," she said.

"We always have time." His tone was so low and erotic that it sent shivers up her spine. The rest of her quivered, too, as his fingers started their quest for her most erogenous zones.

He knew them all now, since several days—and nights—had passed since they first made love. Days when they had been together nearly every moment, as he made good on his promise to protect her. He had trusted no one, not Cal Flynn, not even his own subordinate Snail, to keep her safe.

She *felt* safe in Travis's presence. But that wasn't all she had felt.

They had been together nights, too. He'd made no promises as they shared her bed, but he had satisfied her desire over and over, addicting her so she craved more.

Falling for any man now was sheer foolishness, and

most especially a domineering, controlling, commanding one like Travis. But she couldn't help herself.

She was in love with him.

They slept naked, so she was treated now to the sight of his hard, fully aroused body. The vision, and the way he touched her so erotically everywhere, was too much for her.

"Maybe we have a few minutes," she agreed softly. In moments, he was on top of her, his mouth greedy as he kissed her till she was crazy for more.

And then he entered her, thank heavens. Again. And for the moment, everything else was erased from her mind.

A SHORT WHILE LATER, though, Dianna's thoughts were alert once more. "It's Englander Center's anniversary today," she reminded Travis. "We have to go."

"Yeah," he agreed. "We've got to go. I'm taking you down to San Diego for the day."

"What!" Dianna sat up in bed, clutching the sheet to cover her nakedness. She refused to argue with him while bared to his view. "I'm not going anywhere but to the Center."

"We've talked about this," he growled, turning to reach down to the floor beside the bed. In a moment, he stood and pulled on his boxers. "I agreed that Jeremy shouldn't cancel the celebration, since we don't even know if Farley has anything planned today. But just in case, you won't be there."

Dianna stood on the other side of the bed, still holding the sheet about her. "I'm the Center's manager. I'm in charge of its promotion, in case you don't remember.

Plus, it was named for my husband, who was killed by Farley. I have to be there as Brad's representative. I *will* be there.''

He took a few steps as if planning to grab her. "You will n—"

"You've promised to protect me," she interrupted, refusing to allow him to finish. "That's your job. But keeping me from my responsibilities isn't an option. Now, excuse me while I get dressed."

She met his furious glare with one of her own, but she could see more than his angular face and icy blue eyes as she faced him down. Lord, but the man was sexy, all lean, hard muscle. She knew full well how very male, how sensual, he was.

But her attraction to him…her fledgling love of him…they were irrelevant now.

Of course she was afraid of Farley. She wasn't stupid.

But neither was she a coward. The creep wasn't going to stop her from living her life.

And neither, even for her own safety, would Travis.

WHILE TRAVIS DROVE Dianna's little red sports car down Van Nuys Boulevard toward the Center's parking lot, he stayed alert. Watchful.

Hard to do with the mid-morning crowd forming in the civic center plaza. Street performers were already lined up on the stages erected for the celebration—singers, magicians, other jugglers, mariachis surrounded by colorfully clad dancers.

A grandiose celebration, and a security nightmare.

"Are some of the people on stage yours this time, too?" Dianna asked. Her voice sounded strained. A hell of a woman. She was obviously nervous, but she was here all the same.

Despite his better judgment.

He glanced at her. The pallor of her cheeks complemented the blond hair that framed her face. She was beautiful.

And she drove him nuts. In bed, of course, but most especially by her stubbornness.

"They will be," he responded to her question. "My guys are meeting with me first. I handpicked officers for their abilities to stop crowds in more ways than one."

"Do they know what Farley looks like?"

Travis turned the steering wheel to head the car up the Center's entry ramp. "They all have the composite we put together from your description, plus the composites the feds distributed before. For all the good they'll do. I doubt he'll wander around here looking like himself. He uses disguises."

"I know." Her tone was wry, and also resigned. He felt her turn toward him and slowed the car enough to look at her. "Travis, I don't mean to make your job harder. And I appreciate that you're trying to help me. But I have to be here."

"I know." The hell of it was, he *did* know.

He parked in her reserved space and saw her look nervously around. No wonder. She'd seen Farley right here more than once. He watched her scan other nearby people. "He's not here?"

"No." She sounded relieved.

"So you're ready?"

"As ready as I'll ever be."

They'd already discussed what to do once they'd arrived. They wanted everything to appear as normal as possible, including Travis's cover, assuming Farley hadn't already seen through it—a big assumption.

First, after checking in with Cal Flynn and his all-but-useless security gang, they went outside to Manny's cart. The guy was already busy selling coffee and doughnuts to the group of customers elbowing each other to be first in line, and Travis couldn't help grinning as Dianna offered to help. "Fare to keep you awake and alive." No, *he* would do that, not Manny's stuff.

He himself did a bit of warm-up juggling—as if that relaxed him this time. He saw Dianna watching him from the corner of her eye. He played up the danger of his knife act, just for fun. And because it also got the crowd that surrounded him cheering. But no sign of Farley.

Then they went inside, headed for Dianna's proposed child-care area in the building's bowels. Soon, they were joined by Travis's undercover squad. Many were already dressed and made up as street performers for the occasion. There were enough of them to fill the good-sized basement room, and they jostled each other as they finished getting ready.

Travis, after walking among them, reiterated his orders for the day, reminded them this was the place to assemble before the celebration's big press conference scheduled for early afternoon in the Center's community room. They would share information here. A little later he, too, would don his cover, go out on the promenade and juggle some more, so he left his equipment in a corner here, for easy access.

They headed for Dianna's office.

"You okay?" he asked her in the empty elevator.

"Sure," she lied. "Look, how about if I go out to the plaza for a little while before the press conference. I want to—"

"I know, you want to be visible for the sake of the Center, and your husband." He didn't try to hide his irritability. And it wasn't just because he knew she'd put herself into danger.

He was jealous, damn it. Of a dead man. Her husband.

A U.S. Representative. A politico, well connected, well respected.

Unlike a simple, stupid street cop like him.

Yeah, he'd admitted it to himself somewhere during his last days in Dianna's constant presence. He was definitely involved with the subject of his current mission.

He'd fallen for her. Hard.

But that couldn't make him careless. This time, his subject would not be harmed. Period.

"Yes, my appearance for the Center—and for Brad—is important," Dianna agreed quietly. "And if I just hide, Farley will have won."

Before he could respond, the elevator door opened. Jeremy Alberts stood there with his daughter.

"Why aren't you in school, honey?" Dianna asked Julie.

"Dad promised I could see what was going on. He's taking me to school now, but I'll be back this afternoon, right, Dad?"

Alberts might have been a hard-ass otherwise, but he was a soft touch to his daughter's wishes. His long face that always looked as if he was eating prunes lightened up. "Right," he replied. "And then maybe Dianna could have dinner with us."

Speaking of softness, the look the guy draped over Dianna said it all. Travis wasn't the only one who wanted her. The thing was, he might have her in bed for a few hot, heavy nights, but he wasn't the kind she'd want anything permanent with.

Jeremy Alberts, on the other hand, was more her social caliber.

But Dianna knew the score for now. She was Travis's responsibility. She glanced at him as if seeking permission he couldn't give, not unless he was along to watch over her. But she didn't say no. Probably wanted to keep her options open with the guy. "Let's see how the day goes," she replied.

Right, Travis thought. Let's see if the Center is still standing and we're all alive at the end of this hell of a day.

TRAVIS'S DISCUSSION with Dianna about what was scheduled next ended abruptly when her office door was shoved open. Beth hurried in, saying, "Travis is here with Ms. Englander. But, sir, you should—"

"Is anyone else in these offices right now?" demanded Captain Hayden Lee, head of the LAPD's special undercover "L" Platoon, who followed her.

"No," Beth said. "They're all at the anniversary celebration. But—"

"Good," Lee said, turning to Travis. "I was already on my way up here to find you, Bronson, when I got a call." He waved his cell phone.

Travis had known his boss was likely to be in the area

today keeping an eye on things. He could tell by Hayden's pallor and narrowed eyes that the guy was rattled. "What's wrong?" he asked.

"Come out here. Fast." Hayden, a bulky Asian American whose face was as wrinkled as crumpled paper, pointed Travis into the hallway.

Travis complied, sparing only a glance toward Dianna, whose expression was a mixture of curiosity and trepidation. Beth was by her side, staring indignantly toward the men.

Hayden didn't usually go undercover anymore, but today he wore clothes as casual as any Travis had ever seen him in: a blue cotton shirt and khaki slacks. He didn't waste any words. "We got a bomb scare."

"Damn. What do we know?"

"Guy claiming to be Farley called the Van Nuys station. Said he was pleased to have the opportunity to bring down Englander Center on its first birthday. Gave what he said was an hour's warning. The Deputy Chief stationed at Van Nuys got the word, called me since I'd just stopped in to say hello. They're deploying all available officers. Bomb Squad's on the way."

"That was all he said? I mean, no word about where it'd be, anything? He's liked to brag in the past."

"He didn't say more," Hayden said. "Not even why he's given so much notice. But here's what I want you to do. First thing, get everyone out of here. Then—" He rattled off some orders. Clearly, he didn't care whether Travis's cover was blown now.

Neither did Travis. Still…

Obeying orders was second nature to him. It came naturally after his stint in the military, his years on the force. He protested anyway. He looked his boss in the eye. "I can't do all that, Hayden, and keep Dianna safe. She's my mission."

"Your mission, Bronson," said Hayden, "is Englander Center. Protecting all civilian lives, not just one." He hesitated only a moment. "So you let another one get under your skin? I thought you learned that lesson."

Travis felt as if he'd been pelted with ice kicked up by a Zamboni at an L.A. Kings hockey game. Maybe even skewered with the blades that scored the ice in the first place. "Yeah," he said. "I did. And you're right. Ms. Englander is only part of why I'm here."

He noticed from the corner of his eye that Dianna's office door had opened. She stood there, her lovely, ashen face expressionless as she watched them. Beth was right behind her.

Hayden lifted his thin brows as he looked at Travis, then addressed Dianna. "Sorry for bursting in like that, Ms. Englander. I'll introduce myself later. Right now, we have a situation. Bronson, see you downstairs."

"What is it, Travis?" Dianna asked softly when Hayden had gone. "Did Farley—"

"Yeah, Farley." He glanced at Beth. No use mincing words. "Bomb threat."

Beth gave a little scream. "We need to get out of here." She hurried down the hall.

Dianna didn't move. "Tell me—"

"No time. Now, listen. We're going to evacuate Englander Center. I'll get three of my best men to be with you. Maybe there is actually a bomb set to go off, and that's what I have to find out. But in case it's a ploy to divert attention from you, you're not to be alone for even a second. Understand?"

"Yes." The word issued with no objection from her gently trembling lips. Lips he wanted more than anything to kiss again.

Lips he ignored as he got her moving.

And yet, even as he hustled her from her office, out of the suite that Beth had apparently already vacated, he could have sworn he heard those very enticing, still lips murmur her unspoken protests.

He wanted to shake her.

He wanted to do more than that with her.

But mostly, he prayed she would stay safe.

ONCE AGAIN Dianna stood across the street from Englander Center, worrying whether it was about to blow up. The people surrounding her were different from last time, when the ticking package was left on her desk. Then, she'd been with Jeremy and Wally.

Now, Wally was dead.

Jeremy was with her, though. So were Snail and two other guys, hulking undercover cops whom Travis had introduced so quickly she wasn't sure she'd heard their names. O'Neill and Smith, maybe. Or Olivier and Short. Her bodyguards.

She watched with dismay as people streamed from the site that, only minutes before, had been the inviting locale of a day's pleasant diversion.

Would the Center's reputation ever recover from two bomb scares? Assuming, of course, that the Center remained standing at all after this latest threat.

"I can't believe this," Jeremy fumed beside her. He

glared at the three men he knew were cops. "Why don't you just catch that Farley character? I've heard of ineptitude, but this is the worst."

As the glares of the three cops centered on the man who'd been so kind to Dianna over the past year, she hastily stepped in. "They're doing what they can, Jeremy. But Farley's elusive. Not even the feds have been able to stop him, and I know they've kept their files open since...since Brad was killed."

Jeremy's gaze softened and he put an arm around Dianna's shoulder. She couldn't help comparing the gesture with how it felt when Travis held her for comfort. No, there was no comparison. Jeremy's arms were thin beneath his usual suit jacket, and since he wasn't much taller than she, he had to reach up to clasp her shoulders. His face was long, the look he turned on her morose instead of determined.

"I didn't mean to remind you of that," he said sadly.

"It's okay." Dianna turned, and Jeremy let go slowly, apparently reluctant. All the more reason to move away in reinforcement of what she'd already made clear: she appreciated his caring but wanted no relationship beyond employer-employee.

Facing the Center, she once more saw the bomb detection unit arrive, with its unwieldy looking equipment. They had dogs with them, too, probably trained to sniff out explosives.

This couldn't be happening again.

No, it *was* happening. And this time it might be more than one of Farley's disgusting jokes.

She stared through the rapidly retreating crowd. Where was Travis? Was he safe?

She knew he'd impose himself into the middle of the action. Be wherever the damned bomb was anticipated to be, to stop it.

Behind her, Jeremy asked the cops questions they couldn't answer. "Where do they think the bastard is this time? Who took his call? Did he give any clues where he stuck the bomb?"

Snail's attempt to respond was valiant, though his answers seemed to be only educated guesses. Dianna stepped farther away, distancing herself from the men assigned to protect her, in mind-set if not actual space.

She scanned the retreating crowd for the familiar, hated face of Farley. Looked for his ugly grin. She didn't see it. Not surprising. He probably watched from a distance, enjoying himself while ensuring that he would not be caught.

Bill Hultman approached. She didn't like the chilly smile on the restaurant owner's face. "Two bomb scares in two weeks is disruptive enough for me to get out of my lease, don't you think, Ms. Englander? If the building doesn't blow up, of course. Ever hear of a tenant's right to quiet enjoyment? I'm sure I'll find legal grounds to get out of it now."

He sounded too pleased by the idea. But before Dianna could think of an appropriate response, her cell phone rang. She pulled it from her purse. The caller ID number was Travis's. He'd told her he would call now and then to make sure she was with her bodyguards—and that she was safe.

"Hi," she said eagerly into the receiver. "Where are you? Are you all right?"

A horrible laugh sounded in her ear. "I'm just fine, darling," cackled an all-too-familiar voice.

Farley.

But the phone number was Travis's cell. She was sure of it.

"What do you want?" she demanded coldly, her spine prickling in fear. How had Farley gotten Travis's phone?

"I want you, of course, Dianna," the voice said. "Did you notice the caller ID number before you answered?"

"No," she lied.

"Oh, I bet you did. Why else would you answer that way?"

She remained silent.

"You know whose phone I have. How do you suppose I got it?"

Dianna had the horrible feeling he would tell her whether or not she replied. Where was Travis? He wasn't the kind of person who lost things like his cell phone. He'd know if it was stolen.

Surely Farley hadn't harmed him.

The devil's next words shattered Dianna's prayers. "You don't need to answer, Dianna. I'll tell you. I have Lt. Bronson. He'll die here in Englander Center when my bomb explodes. Won't you just love that? I know he's an undercover cop and that the two of you have spent a lot of time together…under the covers. Isn't that sweet? And now I'll be able to destroy him, just as I did your dear Brad. Would you like to watch again?"

Dianna felt as though she was going to throw up. "Wh—what do you want, Farley?"

"One minute. Let's not rush things. There's someone else here who wants to say hello."

"Dianna!" The shrill child's voice shouted into the phone. "Help me. He came to my school and—"

"You can tell her later." Farley's voice was muffled as if he didn't hold the phone. In a moment, he said, "You know who that is?"

Of course. Julie.

As scared as Dianna was before, now her throat closed in panic. "You bastard," she choked. "Leave her alone."

"I will…probably," said Farley. "It's not my intention to *harm* children, just use them."

"What do you want?" Dianna tried not to sob into the phone.

"You."

Could anyone survive long with a heart racing as hard and fast as hers? Maybe it didn't matter.

She was going to die anyway.

Dianna turned to see what her bodyguards were doing. All three spoke with the angry Jeremy, though their eyes were on her.

Jeremy. What would he do if he knew his daughter was in danger? Should she tell him?

She turned her back again so her expression wouldn't betray her horror. "What do you mean, you want me?"

"You're the only person I worry about these days, Dianna. You've seen me as I really am. I've worn a disguise in front of Julie, so she's no threat, but you can identify the real me to the cops. So, tell you what. You come here, and I'll make a trade. Your life for your dear

Lt. Bronson's and sweet little Julie's. Two for one. What a deal.''

"Let me talk to Travis.'' She wasn't stupid. Even if Farley had Travis, he might already be…dead.

"Nope. He's a little indisposed right now, though I promise you he is alive—at least at this moment. Now, here's what you do. I was there before, you know, when your dear lieutenant met with his undercover troops in that little basement room at the Center. Neither of you recognized me, of course. But that's where I've taken Julie and Bronson. You come here, and I'll make sure *they* get out of Englander Center before it goes boom.''

Dianna took a slow, deep breath. *She* wouldn't get out. That's what he meant. But she couldn't let Travis and Julie die.

She would never be able to live with herself if two people she loved were murdered because of her.

Of course, if she went, *living* with anything would no longer be an issue for her. As if she had a choice.

"All right, I'll come,'' she said softly into the phone.

"Come alone.'' He hung up.

Dianna held her phone to her ear for another long moment, then slowly closed it and put it in her purse.

Behind her, Jeremy was still jabbering to the three police officers. Furtively, she sneaked a look. Snail and the others appeared irritated. Their gazes were on Jeremy.

She knew she should tell them about the call. Let them do something. They were, after all, cops.

But they didn't know Farley. The man was cunning enough, insane enough, to kill Travis and Julie, then still blow up the place and escape. Not that she could stop him. But she knew he wanted *her*. Maybe that would be enough of a statement for him: he killed Brad Englander's widow on the day the center named for him celebrated its first anniversary.

Maybe, by doing as he said, she would be the only victim, and he'd let Julie and Travis go.

And if she were really lucky…maybe she could get him first.

Again, she looked. Were Snail and the other officers distracted enough to let her slip away?

No time like the present to find out.

There were a lot of people around, the crowd evacuating the Center. Quickly, Dianna stepped among them. They were going the wrong way, but she'd double back as soon as she could.

Without another glance to see if she was being observed, she slipped away.

"WHAT DO YOU MEAN she got away?" Travis demanded into the cell phone he'd borrowed to check on Dianna. He'd called Snail first for a report. Explosion? Hell. This news made him feel ready to detonate as fiercely as any bomb the SOB Farley may have planted at the Center.

"She was there one minute talking on her phone. We all had our eyes on her. And then…she was gone." Snail's voice sounded small and contrite. As it should. Travis would bust him for this. All of them.

But that wouldn't protect Dianna.

Travis had the urge to hurl something in his frustration. If it had been his own cell phone, maybe he'd have destroyed it. But when he'd reached into his pocket, his had been gone. He was never careless enough to leave it behind. Had someone taken it? He'd been in more than one shoving crowd that day, but he knew all the sticky finger tricks. He'd used them himself.

But there was no time to deal with a mere annoyance right now. He was inside the Englander Center lobby with the explosives team, and he'd borrowed one of their phones. He was going to call Dianna but decided to first check with Snail.

Good thing he had. What the hell was she thinking? He'd call her in a second to find out, before laying into her but good. First, though…

"Find her." Travis didn't raise his voice but made it damned clear he meant business.

Why hadn't the stubborn woman listened to him just this once?

He couldn't rely on his men to locate her. He *wouldn't* rely on them. Dianna was his responsibility, even if he'd been given conflicting orders.

"Any idea what direction she went?"

"She just disappeared into the crowd, sir," Snail said.

Of course the crowd was heading away from Englander Center. That didn't mean Dianna was.

Had Farley gotten to her? How?

He needed to find her. Fast.

He pressed her number into the cell phone and waited for her to respond.

He nearly jumped out of his skin when the phone stopped ringing. "Dianna?" he shouted. "Where are you?"

"She's with me, Bronson," said a high and whiny male voice. "Care to join us? We're in the Center's basement. See you soon."

And then there was nothing.

Chapter Fifteen

The Glen Farley Dianna knew, the demon who'd murdered Brad in front of her, had a middle-aged face, lined and paunchy.

The man who had faced her at the door of what was to have been her child-care room, who'd grabbed her cell phone from her purse when it rang, appeared years younger—no wrinkles, no sags.

Not even a scar from where she had raked her key down his face only a few weeks ago.

Shock slammed her in the face when she realized she had seen him earlier today, right here in the chilly Englander Center basement during Travis's briefing of his undercover platoon. She'd noticed this guy she'd assumed was one of Travis's cops because he'd looked familiar. Hadn't she seen him before today, too? She hadn't associated him with Farley, though. Why—?

"Please have a seat," he said as if inviting her into his home for a party.

In his own sick way, maybe he was. But the large, ugly pistol he pointed at her belied any hospitable intent.

He wore a T-shirt and blue jeans, as most of the street performers did—those not in costume, at least. He appeared to be in his early twenties, in the dim basement light.

Only the cunningly mad gleam in his eyes told her that this was, in fact, Farley.

"Why do you have to kill me because I can recognize you?" she blurted. "You use disguises most of the time anyway."

"Except when I want you to notice me," he reminded her. "And sometimes I just want to be me without worrying if the cops will catch me."

She didn't bother pointing out that physical description was only one way the authorities could identify him. Logic had never been Farley's forte.

She had no intention of taking her eyes off him or his gun, yet as she obeyed his insistent motion and stepped further into the room she peered into the dimness.

"Dianna!" Julie stood against the far wall, in an area that had been used—was it only an hour earlier?—for Travis's platoon's preparatory meeting. Some officers had changed into their undercover gear there, their costumes for performing. Neat stacks of their belongings littered the floor, not far from the pile of basement debris shoved out of the way into the corner—small pieces of wood, lumps of concrete, a broken tool or two.

Some ad hoc performers had left props for their acts there, too, for later retrieval if necessary.

Like Travis…

In the middle of the floor was something that turned Dianna's blood flow to an icy trickle. It appeared to be sticks of dynamite attached to something resembling a clock.

The bomb that would destroy Englander Center. And everyone who remained inside…

"Where's Travis?" Dianna demanded as Julie raced across the room and into her arms.

"On his way here," Farley told her. "I lifted his cell phone when he gave his pep talk to his sadly recognizable undercover squad before. Fortunately, they added people for today and didn't know one another, just checked identification. Mine looked *so* real. I doubt he noticed when one more person bumped him in that crowd when I 'borrowed' his cell phone from his pocket to call you. Now I've used yours to tell him where to find you. Full circle. You can watch each other die."

"No!" Julie wailed. Her head back, she stared up into Dianna's face with terrified eyes. "I don't understand why Mr. Glen is doing this. When Daddy—"

"Didn't I tell you before that you were to be very quiet unless I told you to talk, Julie?" Farley's voice was low but the menace in it shredded the nerves along Dianna's spine. Julie, trembling against her, began to sob.

Farley was going to kill them all. Travis, too. If only Dianna could warn him, somehow, to stay away.

As if he would.

Dianna admitted to herself that the thought of his being here gave her hope. Maybe he'd think of something to save them.

Maybe he'd die...

Dianna couldn't chance it. She'd come here without telling anyone so she could save Travis as well as Julie. Yet how could she do anything at all while terrified for the child in her arms?

"You've got me," she said woodenly to Farley. "You'll have Travis. There's no need to harm Julie."

"Of course not," he said with a wounded expression on the face that Dianna could now see, despite the gloominess of the poorly-lighted room, was coated with makeup. "I told you I use children. I don't hurt them, as long as they obey me. Especially Julie. Run along now, quietly, young lady. Your dad is probably out there somewhere, right, Dianna?"

"Yes. I left him across the street."

"But Dianna—"

"You can't help me here, honey," she said. "But you can help outside. Make sure the police know what's going on here, okay?"

They already knew, even if they weren't sure where the bomb was, but giving Julie a mission might get her moving quickly.

"Okay," the child said reluctantly. Tears ran down her cheeks as she backed away from Dianna. "Is he going to kill you?"

Dianna shook her head. "I hope not, but I need for you to leave so I can talk some sense into him." As if she could. Her chances of survival were nearly nil, and hated that a lie might be Julie's last memory of her. "I'll see you in a little while."

She sighed in relief as Julie ran out of the room and down the hall in the direction of the emergency stairway.

Would it make any difference if she ran into Travis? Unlikely. He would come here, her knight whose shining armor consisted of snug T-shirt and jeans, and try to save her.

And they both would die.

"How sweet," Farley said when Julie was gone. "But you realize, I'm sure, that you won't be able to 'talk sense into me,' as you called it."

"I know," Dianna acknowledged. "Getting someone else to see reason requires a rational mind to deal with in the first place."

The expression on Farley's falsely youthful face turned ugly. "I know you think I'm mad. But I've always had good reasons for what I've done. Your dear husband hurt me and others. I had to stop him from harming more small businessmen with his miserable plans to put them out of business by redeveloping more perfectly fine areas all over the country that he considered run-down."

"And you saved small businesses by destroying those redevelopments and killing people?"

"Sure. And now I'll have funding to keep going, too. I've found my niche. Killing is fun, and profiting from it, too—well, that's nirvana."

"What do you mean?"

He didn't answer, but used the gun to wave her toward the wall. "Go over there. I need to tie you up, since your lover will arrive any moment."

She slowly obeyed him, her eyes skipping from one possible weapon on the ground to another.

Where, in all the stuff, was what she sought?

When she glanced back at him, he held a rope. He'd have to put the gun down to tie her up. That would be her chance. But where was—

He grabbed her arm, but she dove for the pile of stuff in the corner. All she came up with in that instant was an irregular chunk of concrete. It should be big enough...

She hurled it at his head. He ducked, raising his gun hand and aiming at her.

No. It couldn't end like this. Where was—

"Farley!" A beloved voice sounded from the doorway.

"Travis, look out!" Dianna screamed.

Too late. As Farley turned, he fired toward Travis,

who also held a gun. And then Dianna spotted what she'd been looking for: Travis's things, arranged neatly in a stack along the wall, a closed box at the bottom. She leapt toward the pile and pulled from the box one of his most lethal-looking knives.

When she looked up, she saw Travis stagger into the room, blood on his shirt, his gun hand unsteady.

"No!" She rushed to her feet. Farley had turned at her voice, obviously distracted by waging his war on two fronts.

Dianna took the knife by its hilt and spun it as Travis had taught her, but forward, not up in the air. The blade miraculously hit Farley's gun hand, slicing his wrist open.

With a cry of pain, he fired again, but the shot went wild. He went down in a heap onto the floor as Travis leapt onto him.

How badly was Travis hurt? Dianna couldn't tell. She lifted the concrete rock she'd thrown earlier and stood over the two grunting, fighting men. Farley was on top. Travis must have been weakened by his wound. She prayed he would be all right, even as she took the hunk of concrete and brought it down on Farley's skull. Hard.

The thunk it made told the tale. Farley went slack.

FOR A LONG MOMENT, Travis didn't move. Couldn't move.

His shoulder hurt like hell.

He wasn't sure what Dianna had done, but whatever it was, it had taken care of Farley—for the moment.

Travis rolled so that he, and not Farley, was on top. Bastard. Was he playing possum? Travis checked the man's closed eyes, his pulse. Farley didn't move. Definitely unconscious.

"Did I kill him?" Was that hopefulness in Dianna's voice? Travis couldn't tell. Pain overshadowed his reason just then.

"He's alive." Travis's voice sounded thick even to him. "That's good. I want to see him stand trial."

"He has to pay for all he's done," Dianna agreed.

The jerk still held the rope he'd obviously planned to use on Dianna. Travis felt too weak to be sure he could control the guy, so he rolled him again and tied his hands behind his back, then tested the knots. They held.

He retrieved his knife from the floor, careful to touch only the edges. It would be evidence of what happened here. He glanced admiringly toward Dianna. "We'll turn you into a juggler yet." His words were slurring even more now, damn it.

"We need to find you help," Dianna said. "Let's get out of here."

"Soon," Travis agreed. He slowly drew himself to his feet, then turned to face the bomb. "That thing armed?"

"I don't know." Her voice shook. She stared at him as if he was going to blow apart even as she watched.

Not now. He had too much to do.

Travis hunched over as he loped unevenly toward the bomb. Damn, he hurt. He bent and looked at the nasty contraption. "The timer's not set yet. We can get the explosives guys here."

"Okay. I'll call for help." Dianna, standing over him, reached into her purse for her cell phone.

And then, with a gasp, she fell to her knees. He shook his head to clear it. What was she doing?

Before he could figure it out, she picked up that big concrete rock she'd used before against Farley.

Suddenly, Travis's head was rocked with pain, and everything went dark.

"TRAVIS? TRAVIS, please wake up."

He didn't want to, damn it. He hurt too much. All over. Mostly his head. But how could he resist, with Dianna's sweet voice enticing him?

"Hey, lieutenant. Gotta wake up now."

Startled, Travis opened his eyes. Dianna was there— a couple of her. His vision was blurred. Snail was there, too. They both leaned over him.

What the hell was Snail doing here? And where *was* "here"?

He remembered all at once what had happened. Sort of. He glanced around. They were still in the basement.

"Bomb?" he croaked.

"The Bomb Squad guys have it," Snail replied. "It wasn't set, but if it had been, it could have caused a bit of a mess."

Yeah. Like the end of Englander Center.

Travis started to sit up but was gently pushed back down.

"Hold on there, lieutenant," said an unfamiliar voice, and a uniformed emergency medical technician began to work on him. "Let's count your wounds, shall we?"

Travis only grunted as the pain intensified.

"Will he be all right?" That was Dianna's voice, sounding as if she cared. Maybe this agony was even worth it.

Dianna. This agony. The cement block…

"What happened?" Travis demanded, sitting up. Damn. That hurt like hell.

"You were playing hero, boss," Snail said. "Too bad that turd Farley's dead. He—"

"What do you mean, dead? He's alive. I checked him."

"Not with a slug the size of the San Fernando Valley in his chest."

"But—"

"Just relax," said the EMT.

"He didn't see," said Dianna's voice. "And I don't know who it was. The person was in disguise. He hit Travis over the head, then shot Farley."

"What!" But Travis couldn't quite take it in. The EMT must have drugged him, for he lost consciousness again.

THE NEXT TIME Travis woke up, he was in a hospital. He could tell by the god-awful medical smell and the ugly, sterile stuff surrounding him. He opened his eyes.

"You're awake," Dianna said unnecessarily. But having her there was certainly necessary. She looked like an angel, soft hair falling over her face as she bent her head to look at him. Her pretty blue eyes were narrowed—surely she wasn't worried about him. But those lips he'd loved to taste were smiling.

"You'll be fine," she continued. "The bullet took a chunk out of your shoulder but didn't hit bone. You just need rest."

It all rushed back to him then. "But Farley—"

"You don't have to worry about him now. None of us do."

Travis struggled to sit up. Damn it all, there was a needle stuck in his arm, an IV. He hated needles. "He was alive."

"No, Travis," Dianna said gently. "He's dead."

That brought him fully awake. He scowled. "He was alive," he repeated. "I checked him."

"The person who hit you over the head grabbed Farley's gun from the floor and shot him."

"What? Who?" This made no sense. Travis had wanted the guy alive, so he'd stand trial, suffer knowing that he'd be punished for the ugly stuff he'd done. And he'd been alive.

He remembered a little more now. Dianna's lifting a lump of concrete from the floor. The pain.

What had Dianna said? "He has to pay for what he's done."

He'd thought she was agreeing that Farley had to stand trial. Instead... What had she done?

He reached out and grabbed Dianna's arm. Something on his face must have told her he'd remembered, for her eyes widened. She looked afraid.

"Why did you kill him, Dianna?" Travis demanded.

A BRAND-NEW NIGHTMARE. That was all Dianna could think a while later as she remained in Travis's hospital room. They weren't alone. His boss, Captain Hayden Lee had joined them. The senior policeman looked as grim as Travis did.

At first she'd believed Travis was hallucinating. Now she knew better.

"It's true," she told them. Too upset to sit, she paced Travis's tiny room, edging past Captain Lee in the stiff chair beside Travis's bed. "Someone rushed in the door and hit Travis over the head with something. I grabbed the nearest thing I could, a piece of concrete, since Travis had taken back his knife and Farley's gun. I wasn't fast enough. As Travis lost consciousness, whoever it was grabbed the gun and shot Farley."

"And your description of this mysterious stranger was

what?'' Dianna cringed once more at the cynicism in Travis's voice.

"He wore all black, including gloves, and had a ski mask over his face. It happened so fast that I can't tell you more.''

"Yeah.''

The moisture in Dianna's eyes threatened to spill over at Travis's continued cynicism, but she refused to let it.

One horror in her life was over. Farley was dead.

But now Travis was trying to hang her for it. Accusing her of murdering an unconscious man.

And she'd no proof her story was true.

"And what had you just said about Farley a little earlier?'' Travis asked. Again. They were rehashing details in front of his boss now, but this was the third or fourth time they had gone over it all.

"I said he had to pay for all he'd done,'' she whispered.

She saw the glance that passed between Travis and Hayden Lee.

How could Travis believe that of her? He knew her better than that, didn't he?

Not really. They'd been good in bed together. But he'd never indicated that their apparent relationship was anything more than maintaining his damnable cover.

He'd berated her over and over for not following his orders. She'd done what she'd needed to maintain her dignity. To survive.

She'd fallen in love with another domineering man. But this one didn't love her back.

Instead, he believed her a murderer.

She could almost feel the handcuffs on her wrists....

"I'm sorry you don't believe me,'' she said. "I can't prove that what I've said is true. But you can't prove it isn't, either. I admit I hated Farley, but I didn't kill him.''

Slowly, she walked from Travis's hospital room, leaving a piece of her heart there with him.

Chapter Sixteen

Two days had passed since the anniversary fiasco.

Two days in which Dianna couldn't sleep, hardly ate, and cringed each time the phone rang, both here in her office and at home.

Not that she expected any more hang-ups, or messages, from Farley.

It was late evening now, dark outside her windows. Dark inside *her*. She should go home. Why? To listen to her messages there as she just did here?

Why bother?

She straightened papers on her already neat desk. It had been hard over the past days to concentrate on work, but, then, there had been little work for the manager of Englander Center to do. After a second bomb threat, the public wasn't exactly waiting in line to come here for alternate dispute resolution.

She'd just replayed nearly a dozen messages. Two were cancellations. None had been from prospective customers. Most were the media.

Three were from Travis,

Though her heart leapt at the sound of his voice, his assurance that he was doing well, she had refused to call him back. He wanted to talk to her, he said.

Why? To interrogate her further about how he believed she killed Farley when he was unconscious? Dianna shut her eyes as pain surged through her again.

She had lowered her guard, permitted herself to care again for a man who was sure he should be in charge, that everyone should take orders from him.

And since she didn't meekly comply, he considered her capable of murder.

The media had picked up on the idea. Though they had dutifully reported her story of an "alleged" masked assailant who'd administered Farley's finishing shot, it was obvious no one bought it.

Media coverage had been vile. The whole horror of Brad's murder was rehashed over and over on television, the radio, newspapers. Even the most objective commentators seemed to assume she'd jumped on the opportunity to avenge Brad's death. Dianna expected to see even more when the next issues of weekly news magazines were published.

She particularly wasn't looking forward to the way the tabloids would sensationalize the whole thing.

Over and over, she replayed the scene in her mind. Who could it have been? Farley had hinted in his calls at being paid this time for his threats. The only person she could think of who would believe he'd benefit from the destruction of Englander Center was Bill Hultman. She hadn't been able to bring herself to talk to him, but—

Her phone rang again. She let it roll over into voice mail. And then, since it would be her last call before she left for home, she listened to the message.

"Dianna, it's Travis. I'm coming over right now. I know you're still there, so wait for me."

Sure she would. Just like she'd welcome him with open arms.

She was aware he'd been released from the hospital only today. He would know she was still at her office since he'd ordered his men to continue to keep an eye on her. She saw Snail around a lot, talking to Beth, as usual. But he wasn't there to flirt. This time, his presence wasn't for Dianna's protection, either. It was undoubtedly to see if she'd do something to give herself away, prove she'd murdered Farley.

Maybe to keep her from fleeing L.A.

She sighed and removed her purse from a bottom desk drawer. She wasn't a quitter. And flight wouldn't diminish her current notoriety.

A knock sounded on her open office door. Startled, she looked up. Had Travis gotten here so soon?

No, it was Jeremy. "I thought I still heard you here," he said. "How are you doing, Dianna?"

"Fine," she lied.

His morose eyes slid over her. She figured he saw through her fib. She'd put on one of her nicest business pantsuits this morning—charcoal, with a beige silk shirt—but it seemed to hang on her. When she had last refreshed her makeup, it hadn't done much to hide the dark circles beneath her eyes or the gauntness in her cheeks.

"I'm glad," he said. He stepped inside and leaned against the door, straightening his suit jacket. "Care to join me for dinner?"

"Not tonight, thanks." Then, to change the subject, Dianna asked, "How's Julie?"

"Resilient, thank heavens. She's at a friend's house right now working on a school project. I'll pick her up soon. She was so scared when we finally found each other outside the Center that day, so afraid you were going to die. Fortunately, Beth saw her first and kept her safe until we located one another.''

"That bastard Farley told me right in front of her that he intended to kill me." Iciness inched its way up Dianna's back once again, but she refused to let the horror get to her any longer. She was alive. And safe—at least from Farley. He'd never stalk her again.

"It's been hard on you, hasn't it? I'm very sorry. But it'll be over soon."

"It *is* over," she said firmly. "The police won't be able to prove I killed Farley because I didn't."

"Of course. Tell you what. If you can stand going back downstairs, come to the basement with me now and show me your plan to develop the child-care center. Though it may be gruesome to say, the company is getting some insurance proceeds from poor Wally's death, and I want to use it for your nursery."

"Really? That's kind of you, Jeremy."

"No, it's good business." But the way he looked at her, expectation of some sort written all over his face, made her uneasy. She thought she'd let him down gently enough, made it clear that she was not attracted to him. If he funded her project, maybe he'd feel she would have to do something in return, like show some interest in him.

But the project had merit. And he was right. It *was* good business. Might even draw people back to Englander Center…eventually.

"Sure," she told him, vowing to make clear again, at an appropriate moment, that she would not date him. "I'll show you what I have in mind."

Of course Travis was on his way here. Cal Flynn's

security team would let him into the building, but he would see she hadn't waited for him.

The idea of seeing him again, even so he could interrogate her, sent a pang of longing through her.

Foolish woman.

Jeremy and she talked about trivialities on the elevator ride down to the lobby: Julie's schoolwork. Jeremy's plans for A-S in the future. He and Wally had been discussing ideas for their next development project before Wally's death. People with proposals had been parading through the A-S offices for weeks.

In the lobby, they got on an elevator in a separate bank for the journey to the basement.

And as the door opened on the dimly-lighted underground area, Dianna stifled a gasp.

She remembered now where she had seen the person Farley had last been, in his disguise here in the basement where he had died.

In the A-S office suite.

He'd been there one day after school when Julie had been around. When she'd mentioned him as Mr. Glen when she was held captive down here, mentioned her dad, it hadn't been because Farley had introduced himself that horrible day.

Julie knew him.

Jeremy knew him.

But—

"Come inside, Dianna," Jeremy said. His calm voice had suddenly taken on a note of menace.

"You know, I forgot that Travis is meeting me upstairs. I'd better—"

"You'd better come here." Jeremy took her arm. She tried to pull away gently, but his grip tightened like a vise.

"Please, Jeremy. I need to go."

"What you need is to stay here." He yanked on her arm, and she stumbled into the dank, gloomy room that was to be transformed into her child-care center.

She drew in her breath at what she saw in the faint illumination. In the center of the floor sat the same kind of contraption that had been there two days earlier.

A bomb.

"What's this about, Jeremy?" she asked, trying not to allow him to lead her farther into the room. But despite his greater age and his apparent slightness, he was strong. He shoved her so she nearly hit the closest wall.

"It's about Englander Center," he said. "And about you, and my wife and Glen Farley." He pointed a gun at her. Where had it come from? Not that it mattered. He aimed it at her heart.

"I…I don't understand," Dianna whispered, her eyes on his weapon.

"You know Farley came to see me in the A-S offices a couple of times in disguise, don't you? If you didn't recall it before, I figured you would eventually."

Dianna leaned against the wall for support as her mind raced. Maybe she could get Jeremy to explain. "I remembered seeing him with the same makeup on that he wore down here," she admitted. "But how did you know him?"

"It wasn't easy tracking him down when all those law enforcement agencies failed after he killed Brad. But I enticed *him* to come to *me*. There are those magazines for mercenaries, and I placed a rather well-worded ad. Since you do promotional work, you'd be proud of how I did it—couched in trivialities yet obviously aimed at telling him I'd pay him to get the revenge he himself wanted."

"Against me?"

"Of course."

"But why?"

"It's your own fault." There was no pleasantness in Jeremy's tone or on his face now. His ugly scowl suggested he was ready to pull the trigger. "You had to make Englander Center your own. Come down here and develop your wonderful idea of a child-care center. But as soon as you started, tried to pull permits, the truth would have been revealed. In fact, I'm surprised you didn't already suspect it." He pointed behind Dianna.

Slowly, carefully, she turned to look. The only thing behind her were the room's concrete walls— a bit damp-looking, a few cracks... Cracks! "Is the Center's foundation unstable, Jeremy?" she asked quietly.

"Then you did suspect it! I thought so."

She didn't bother to tell him that, though the basement had its problems, she hadn't thought they extended to the entire building. Until now.

And then something else he'd said made sense. "Your wife—Millie—she worked for the City's permit department here in Van Nuys. Was she aware you cut corners when you built the Center?"

"Not at first, but when she figured it out, she threatened to tell her brother Wally. That's why she had her 'accident' on the stairway at our home. Fortunately, Wally hadn't guessed what I'd done, either in cutting corners at the Center or to his sister. He caught me, though, when I put the ticking clock on your desk, but I even got out of that—at first—by saying it was a joke, for publicity for the Center. But that made him suspicious, and then he barged into my office when Farley was there meeting with me. That meant he had to die like his sister. I had to trick Wally, set it up with Farley to do the dirty work.''

Set up. That was what Wally had tried to tell her, not ''upset.''

Jeremy walked to the edge of the room and bent down without taking the gun off her. Was he picking something up?

''Anyway,'' he continued, ''I got Farley to come here so he'd have his fun disposing of you, and I'd pay him a little something besides. I wanted him to blow up the Center, so I'd get the insurance money. It needed to be done soon, since we didn't build the place to withstand even a moderate earthquake. I bought plenty of special insurance, though, and with the proceeds I'd be able to rebuild and do it right. But I couldn't take the chance that you'd figure out the problem in the first place.''

He approached her now, obviously hiding something behind his back in one hand while he kept the gun trained on her with the other.

''Jeremy, please,'' Dianna said. ''Maybe we can get some funding to fix the problems. Or—''

He brought his hand forward. It contained a hypodermic syringe. She shuddered. He was going to plunge it into her, filling her with…what? Something to knock her out? Poison?

It didn't matter, for when he set off the bomb, she would die anyway.

Travis, her mind called. Had he come here as he'd promised? She wanted him out of the building, so he wouldn't die, too.

She wished she could see him one more time, to explain—

''You were the man dressed in black who killed Farley!'' Dianna blurted.

"Of course." Jeremy sounded as if that was the most obvious observation of all. He reached out with the hand holding the hypodermic. "Now, it's time for you to rest so I can set the bomb's timer. Goodbye, Dianna."

He was fairly close to her now. With strength born of desperation, she kicked upward, expecting to feel pain as the gun went off. Instead, she heard his grunt of pain as the toe of her shoe connected with his groin.

"You bitch!" He was doubled over for just a moment, then lunged at her.

She heard the gun go off and waited for the agony to begin—or for nothingness to overtake her.

Instead, she saw Jeremy slump to the floor, a bright red spot appearing on his chest.

"Dianna! Are you all right?" Travis hurried into the room. He was limping.

Her knees went weak. She leaned against the wall as he checked Jeremy. "He's still alive," Travis called toward the door. Snail hurried in, followed by a couple of other familiar cops, and even Cal Flynn. "Take care of him," Travis told Snail. "And one of you call the explosives team again. I'm getting damn tired of finding bombs around here."

And then Dianna was in Travis's arms. "When are you going to listen to me?" he demanded huskily. "You didn't answer my calls. I wanted to apologize for doubting you. I wanted—"

"But you didn't know till now that I was telling the truth. Or do you know it even now? Did you hear Jeremy?"

"I heard him," Travis said, his blue eyes icy in the dim basement light. But then they warmed as he gazed into hers. "I admit I didn't know it was *him* till now, but I knew you didn't murder Farley almost from the moment I said it. You're not a cold-blooded killer, even to get revenge.''

''Then why did you—?''

''I was angry with myself for letting you get into such danger. I could have lost you. I was unconscious, damn it, and Farley, or whoever murdered him, could have killed *you*.''

She opened her mouth to respond, only to have Travis bend down and silence her with his own.

She had nothing else to say after that—nothing that could even come close to competing with Travis's heated, hungry, highly welcome kiss.

Chapter Seventeen

A week went by.

Travis waited in a joint too grungy to be deemed a restaurant. It was located on Temple Street in downtown L.A., not far from Parker Center, the LAPD headquarters. The food was decent, so cops came here often. He hunched over a cup of coffee on the wood table sanded thin to eliminate initials and comments gouged in by patrons over time. His boss, Captain Hayden Lee, had asked to meet him there.

He didn't like just sitting. It gave him too much time to think.

About Dianna.

Jeremy had died the day Travis shot him. Travis had tried calling Dianna at home the day after that and just got her machine. Just in case, he tried her office. He got a real person this time—Beth. She told him Dianna had taken Julie away for a while, someplace far from where they could be bombarded by the media.

The kid's only remaining blood relations, apparently, were cousins in Delaware she hadn't even met. Travis didn't want to feel for her, but he did. At least Dianna was trying to protect the poor kid. Julie wouldn't have to suffer a childhood like his, lost in the foster system. Not with Dianna on her side.

Though the cops had sat on the truth, newshounds had leapt immediately into not-so-wild speculations about the death of Jeremy Alberts so soon after he had so heroically saved his employee Dianna from her stalker.

That had been the sanitized version of the story of Farley's demise that was leaked to the press.

But neither sanity nor sanitization worked when word got out how Jeremy was actually shot. Travis figured Cal Flynn was the one to leak the truth. Maybe the son of a bitch was even paid by the media to spill it.

The sleazy security company manager had been hand-picked by Farley, recommended to his buddy Jeremy. At least that was Travis's speculation, for Farley and Flynn had known each other years ago in Philadelphia, before Farley had lost his business. Was Flynn intentionally and lucratively inept, or was he chosen for his stupidity? Who knew?

He claimed he hadn't seen Farley in years, and maybe he hadn't, if Farley stayed in disguise while scamming his way into the building with fake ID.

In any event, Flynn's company had been replaced before Dianna disappeared. Beth kept an eye on things at A-S in her absence. Travis had wondered for a while if the curious, flirtatious receptionist had an agenda of her own—like abetting Farley. On questioning, she admitted to having acted suspiciously because of her own burgeoning concerns—about her bosses' work and their acquaintances who passed through the A-S offices. She'd been afraid to say anything, unsure who to trust. Even Dianna had seemed to be great friends with Wally and Jeremy.

Beth had kept notes of her worries in an intentionally

mislabeled file on her computer. She had been horrified to learn her computer had been turned on the day of Wally's murder and her file deleted. Jeremy must have known about it and told Farley. Fortunately, Beth had backed it up on a floppy disk she carried with her. When she'd figured out that Snail just might be an undercover cop, she'd tested him to see if she dared trust him. Now, she did. Not just with her suspicions and her computer disk, but also as her dinner companion, and more. Often. And well, from the way Snail blushed at her name.

In any event, the case was closed. Travis's mission was accomplished. The threat to destroy Englander Center by bomb was stopped. By earthquake was another matter.

For now, even that jerk Bill Hultman was happy, basking in Englander Center's notoriety. His restaurant was packed. He regaled his curious customers with lurid tales of his role in the tale—greatly embellished. He made himself out as both hero and near-martyr. Good for business.

Good for keeping his bitching to a minimum, too.

Most of all, Dianna's stalker was thwarted. Travis had even saved her life, which was his job.

End of story.

After that kiss—apparently her version of a polite thank-you note—Dianna had disappeared from his life without a word.

It was better that way. Quick. Clean. No regrets.

Yeah.

"Hey, Travis, sorry to keep you waiting." His chunky boss Hayden Lee slid into the booth across from him. He signaled a bored-looking waitress, then ordered coffee and a piece of cheesecake.

"No problem. What's up?"

"Two things. I've put you in for a commendation for your work on the Englander matter. Good job."

"Thanks." He wasn't about to mention that doing such a good job had made him feel the greatest pain he'd ever suffered in his life. Limp, hell. His earlier injuries were like nothing. Now, he was an amputee. His damned heart had been torn right out of him and he hadn't even tried to stop it.

Well, yeah, he had. As if he'd been able to keep his emotions from wrapping around Dianna.

He'd survived worse, like getting the subject of a mission whom he'd cared about killed. Dianna was alive.

Only *he* was dead. Inside.

"You okay?" Hayden asked. His coffee and cake had been served, and he pushed the plate with the sweet on it toward Travis. "Looks like you can use some of this."

Travis ignored the cake. "What else did you want to see me about?"

"I have another mission for you. You up for it?"

Hell, yes. He was ready for anything that would get his mind off Dianna. Almost. "Tell me."

"THANKS, JOAN." Dianna waved at the lawyer as she exited her office. She didn't have far to go to her own office—just down a floor, for the family lawyer she'd hired was located in Englander Center.

She pushed the button to call the elevator. The hallway was empty, but she knew there was an arbitration going on in one of the conference rooms. And a trial proceeding on another floor.

With luck, Englander Center would survive.

There were a lot of legal issues to think about, though. Young Julie Alberts was her father's only heir, and Jeremy had inherited all other interests in A-S Development on the deaths of his wife Millie and Wally Sellers. Of course, since he'd killed them, there was some question as to his right to inherit. But in this case, Julie would have been her mother's heir if Jeremy wasn't. And Wally had no kin left, either, after his sister Millie died.

Julie was too young to run the business, of course, so a determination had to be made whether to sell it or to hire someone to manage it for her. Dianna knew enough about it to run it, if the court approved.

More important, she was petitioning the court for permanent guardianship of Julie.

The child's only living relatives were some distant cousins she hadn't even met. Dianna had spoken with them, explained the situation, promised to fly them out to California and do anything necessary to convince them that she was the right person to care for their young, wounded cousin.

She thought she'd heard relief in their voices. She was optimistic that she would be able to convince both them and the court that she could take care of Julie.

She had been taking care of her since her daddy died.

One of the hardest things Dianna ever had to do was telling Julie, that evening, that Jeremy was dead.

Worse, she had to prepare the child for all the allegations against her father that would appear in the media. She couldn't shelter the child from every source of sensationalistic news. And even if she managed to protect Julie from the blitz, her classmates would hear and ask questions. The meanest might even tease her about it.

That was one reason they had gone away, to let the lurid headlines play out until something else captured the reporters' attention.

She had taken Julie back to her class at Beverly Pacifica School that morning, with a warning to Pearl

Kinch, the principal, that all teachers were to be instructed to be alert to anyone taunting the child. If Julie felt anything but welcomed back, she would be pulled out fast. And Dianna would see to it personally that all parents whose kids attended the elite, expensive school were made aware that it did not do enough to shelter its students.

She was issuing orders these days every bit as commandingly as Travis.

Travis.

The empty elevator arrived, and Dianna got in. But she wasn't yet ready to return to her office and all the problems of keeping A-S Development and Englander Center going. Thank heavens for the underappreciated, overachieving Beth.

Automatically, Dianna pressed the button for the ground floor. She'd stop and say hi to Manny. Grab a cup of coffee and perhaps a bagel.

And just maybe, he would have some news of Travis....

Her mind had been on Travis a lot over the past weeks. Heck, she hadn't stopped thinking about him.

She was in love with him.

But with all that had happened—her loss of two men she had cared about personally and professionally, Wally and Jeremy, the terror she'd undergone from Farley and from Jeremy, the shock of learning Jeremy had murdered his wife, plus seeing all three men die...

She'd needed time to breathe.

She had needed also to be with Julie with no distractions. Or at least no tangible, actually present distractions.

And she also could not face, just then, the most likely scenario. She'd been Travis's assignment. He had done what he was supposed to— protect her. Save Englander Center and keep Farley from blowing up any more redevelopment areas in L.A. He'd told her all along that he'd no intention of getting involved with her, though he hadn't been entirely successful about that.

Their lovemaking—physical involvement—had been phenomenal. Yet, he had been partially successful, for she was sure he hadn't gotten emotionally involved.

He had never promised her otherwise.

At the ground floor, she glanced toward the building's entry, where people were being screened by a new security company. She'd fired Cal Flynn's group immediately. They hadn't stopped Farley's entry, over and over. Not that she was surprised now, after learning that Cal Flynn had once been Farley's business associate.

She turned toward the exit doors and stopped. She wasn't sure whether to laugh or cry.

Travis was out there beside Manny's cart, juggling his knives.

Without thinking, she hurried outside. She shared a grin with Manny, then watched

"Heard you were back," Travis said without missing a beat. He was dressed in his habitual snug T-shirt and flesh-hugging jeans. His knives whirled over and over as his hard, sexy muscles pulsated from his activity. He met her eyes, and his smile was challenging.

What was he asking?

"Yes, and I see you're back, too." Why? she wanted to ask. Was he still undercover here for some reason?

As if he'd heard her unspoken question, he said, "New assignment." He caught the knives, one by one, and held them in his hands. "Want to hear about it?"

"Sure." Being in his presence again made her feel giddy.

No, she wanted to cry. To laugh.

Mostly, she wanted to fling herself into his arms.

Instead, she just walked beside him, her head down, not meeting his eyes. Friends could accompany friends on a stroll, after all. And she didn't want him to think she wanted anything else from him.

"So tell me about this new assignment," she said.

"Yeah. I want your opinion."

"Really?" She didn't mean to, but she looked into his face. His grin was full of confident arrogance. Yet she thought she saw something else, too, hidden in the narrowing of his eyes. Surely, it wasn't uncertainty. Not from this brash, commanding man.

They turned the corner onto the mall that bisected the Van Nuys Civic Center. Around them were courthouses and the library, and at the end of the mall was the police station.

Midday like this, the sidewalk was crowded with jurors on breaks and others with business in the San Fernando Valley's main government seat.

A musician played an amplified guitar nearby, and the aroma of warm cinnamon buns from a peddler's cart wafted about them.

They walked slowly as Travis said, "It's like this. I've been in the field a long time. Don't get me wrong. I like the undercover stuff. And I'd never give up juggling or magic. But my boss has made his decision definite. He was offered a promotion, and he's taking it. That leaves his slot open, as head of the whole 'L' Platoon of the LAPD Metro Division. He wants me to take it."

"And what do you want?" Dianna's heart was pounding. It sounded a whole lot less dangerous than being in the field. She liked it.

And if they'd truly been involved, she would have begged him to take it.

But they weren't involved.

"I figure it's a good career move for a guy who's thinking about settling down. Maybe getting married."

"Oh?" Damn, this hurt. Had he been committed to someone else without telling her? "I didn't realize you were in a relationship."

"No? Well, I intend to be." He moved so that he was in front of her. Beside them, the guitarist began to play a soft, sweet love song.

Travis waved his hands in one of his sleight-of-hand gestures. Dianna expected to see a deck of cards appear.

Instead, it was a small, square box.

Travis got down on his knees in front of her. "Dianna, would you do the honor of marrying me?" He opened the box.

Inside, a diamond engagement ring sparkled in the Southern California sunlight. Or was it the tears in Dianna's eyes that gave the stone such a glow?

Dianna sensed, rather than saw, the people on the mall stop and surround them.

She knew what she wanted to say. But there were things he had to know. "I'm trying to adopt Julie," she said, reaching down and drawing him to his feet.

She stood very close to him, so she had to look up into his eyes. One arm went around her, and with his other hand he took hers and pressed the box into it.

"No sweat," he said. "I want kids. And I think the world of Julie."

"And I'm trying to straighten out the mess of who owns or runs Englander Center."

"Your call."

"And then there's the matter of the Center's construction. Because it's a valuable asset to the community, I've been looking into getting a government subsidy to reinforce it, and I'll probably have to figure out how to break leases to empty the place while the work is being done. That's assuming it can be fixed at all. The whole thing is a huge, ugly mess and will probably take a lot of my time.''

"If anyone can manage it, you can.''

She smiled ironically. "You mean, you're not going to tell me what to do about it, issue me orders?''

"Sure I am. Dianna Englander, you are going to marry me. Soon. We'll take care of Julie together, and we'll have a kid or two of our own. What do you say to that?''

"Yes," she said very simply, then pulled his head down into a kiss.

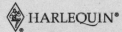

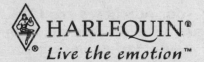

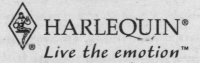

JASMINE CRESSWELL

Art gallery owner Melody Beecham was raised in the elite
social circles of her English mother, Rosalind, and her American
father, Wallis Beecham, a self-made millionaire. But when
her mother dies suddenly, a shocking truth is revealed:
Wallis is not Melody's father. Worse, he is a dangerous man.

And now a covert government agency known as Unit One
has decided to recruit Melody, believing her connections
will be invaluable in penetrating the highest political
circles. They will stop at almost nothing to have
Melody become one of them....

DECOY

"Cresswell skillfully...portrays characters who will interest
and involve the reader."
—*Publishers Weekly* on *The Conspiracy*

*Available the first week of
February 2004 wherever
paperbacks are sold!*

Return to the sexy Lone Star state with *Trueblood, Texas*!

Her Protector
by
LIZ IRELAND

Partially blind singer Jolene Daniels is being stalked,
and Texas Ranger Bobby Garcia is determined to
help the vulnerable beauty—and to recapture
a love they both thought was lost.

Finders Keepers: Bringing families together.

Available wherever books are sold in March 2004.

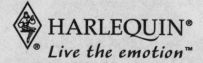

Visit us at www.eHarlequin.com

CPHP

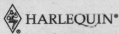

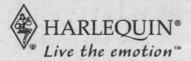

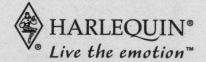